Long Gun

Day Of Consequence

A Distorted Historical Caricature
Of Events In California & The Old West

By
Tony Sanders

For my friends
Ronnie & Marilyn —
"Pards for life!"
Calico 2014

All characters appearing in this work are fictitious.
Any resemblance to real persons, living or dead,
is purely coincidental.

ISBN: 978-1-62050-736-0

Sacrare!

I Dedicate This Book To
Honey Mustard
&
The Few Who Read It First.

Li Sanders, Becky Sanders, Maret Kunze,
Bob Hughes, Lisa Fluor, Rasika Reichardt,
Elizabeth Wenger, Chicki Mallan, Val Martin,
Alexander Sanders, Owen Kent Sanders,
Thom Moore, Tian Qing

Occasionally for no apparent reason, triggered by an unlikely force, over the saga of time, a chain of events will unfold. They carry on of their own accord, forging ahead from their own momentum, until they culminate, on their own terms.

Samuel "Shorty" Small - 1863

July 1, 1876

Hot dry days . . . In the deep summer quiet and brilliant ivory vista of Central California, two hundred miles north of the Pueblo de Los Angeles, ten miles west of the railroad's Coaling Station-A, crouched a bright, arid, dot of a town named San Benito.

Five-year-old Jimmy Longhon crawled on his hands and knees along the rows of semi shade, pulling weeds, and pushing cool, damp soil up around the corn stocks in Polly's yard. Polly was the oldest resident of San Benito, and perhaps all of California. Jimmy listened precociously to the wrinkled old woman as the two of them tended her garden.

"Which cookies do you prefer, Jimmy, Oatmeal or plain sugar?" Polly asked as she worked. Her voice had a wonderful deep timbre. Jimmy found the pitch and resonance, comfortable, warm, and inviting.

The little boy had a soft tan face, blue eyes, white hair and an air of innocence unusual in the unpredictable wilderness of the early American west.

With his inquisitive personality Jimmy stood out among the other five year old children in San Benito.

He thought of everyone in San Benito as family even though they really weren't. He loved to help old Polly Reiner work in her garden. Probably because he lived so close, he was the only child around town who ever came by to visit the old woman. She had grown ninety gardens during her hundred and three years of life. Jimmy had seen only five of them.

"I think I like oatmeal cookies best," Jimmy smiled. "But I've got to get goin'." He said as he stood up, dusting his pudgy little hands on his pants, "Pretty soon Cisco's picken' me up on his way back to his ranch. But I'll come and see ya on the fourth of July. That's America's birthday ya know."

With a cookie in each hand, affectionate gratitude twinkling from her eyes, Polly bent down for Jimmy's hug. "I know honey. America's a hundred and I'm a hundred and three, a few years older than America. Can you believe that?" She handed her little helper two large oatmeal cookies she had made the night before.

"Wow! Is it your birthday on the fourth of July too?" He clamped one of the cookies in his teeth, reached up, closed his eyes warmly, and hugged her arm with his dirty little hand.

"No honey, I think my birthday was in June. Maybe the sixth but the old bible with the day I was born written in it is so faded and dirty I can't read the day clear enough to know for sure. But the year I was born is as clear as can be, 1773. Isn't that a great year?"

Feeling the soft skin of her wrinkled face, he removed the cookie from his mouth, puckered and gave her a kiss including some crumbs from his lips to her cheek. He toddled out of the garden thinking about what she had asked. He turned to wave a cookie holding hand. "Yea. That was a swell year to be born. Bye! See ya on the fourth of July!"

Nestled between Polly's house and Jimmy's was his second favorite place in the world: the hardware store.

Jimmy spent countless hours eye level with the counter-top, paying earnest attention, always hoping to help Ohma Mintz. On the walk home from gardening he couldn't help but stop in to see Ohma. Walking through the door he piped up, "Hey Ohma," in his high-pitched voice. He thought Ohma was her given name. Jimmy didn't know that Ohma meant 'grandmother' in German. He liked to listen to his shoes clonk on the wooden floor as he walked through the deep maze of lofty shelves. He carefully scrutinized all the tools and interesting hardware-store thing-a-ma-bobs on display for little boys. He finally arrived at the counter, all the way at the back of the store, where Mrs. Mintz waited.

"I can't stay long. My mom's letting me go out to Cisco's to help make bricks," he informed the tall, white haired woman. She could just barely see the top of his bright blond head on the other side of her counter. There was no mistaking that he was there. After a moment's pause he lifted up on his toes. His eyes peeked over the edge of the counter smiling with a half eaten cookie in each hand.

"Where'd you get those cookies?" Ohma asked with a feigned look of hunger.

"Polly gave 'em to me." he squeaked holding one out. "Want one?"

Mrs. Mintz took one and gave it a little nibble, "Mmmmmm that's good isn't it, Honey?"

"Yep. Bye!" he said smiling to himself, waved, and trotted all the way back out thru the front door.

At home, Jimmy's mother packed a change of clothes into one side of an old worn out pair of saddlebags that Jimmy used for a suitcase.

Dora Longhon was born Callidora Stewart Emerson in Knoxville, Tennessee and spoke with a distinct southern accent, "You be a good boy out there at Cisco's," she drawled to her son. "And don't get too dirty." Her eyes rolled in her head as she realized the futility of her ridiculous demand. He's a five-year-old boy. Short of an inadvertent bath from falling in the creek, he would be getting dirty.

Cisco (Francisco Hernandez), a kind old Mexican grandfather and Jimmy's favorite friend, farmed vegetables and made adobe bricks on a small plot of land along the depot trail, four miles east of San Benito.

The boy's earliest memories were of Cisco and Lupito, the draft mule, standing outside the fence of his yard. They stopped by everyday when they were in town to look in on the single mother and to play cowboys-and-Indians with Jimmy before they headed back to their ranch.

Even though the dangers of the Wild West were obvious to even the greenest green horn, it only took a little common sense to know which of one's friends could be trusted with one's children. In San Benito, Cisco was known and trusted far and wide. On special occasions Jimmy's mother let the boy ride out with Cisco to play with the old man's grandchildren.

Cisco and Lupito pulled up parallel to the Longhon's front fence. "¡Hola! Dora." Cisco smiled at Jimmy's mother, with his bright, wide, grin that had lots of teeth.

"¡Hola," she replied with her southern accent.

"Hey Cisco! Hey Lupito!" Unimpressed, the mule turned his head to look at Jimmy, and then blew air through his lips.

Cisco graveled his best silly voice for his little friend. "Hey Jeemeeeee!"

Jimmy's mom lifted him over the buckboard rail. He quickly scuffled over the weathered bench to sit next to Cisco.

"Oh my Cisco, this is so nice of you." she worried out loud; "If he gives you any trouble, just give him a good swat on the bottom. I'll see you both back here on the fourth for the celebration." And so the three of them, if you're counting Lupito, trundled away in the wagon.

On very special days, riding far out from town, Cisco let Jimmy hold his "pistolé" and pretend to shoot it. The old man would recite audacious fables of the Spanish Conquistadors and Highwaymen who marched north on foot through California with the padres in long columns of people, horses, goats and cattle.

Jimmy couldn't remember his own father. And he treasured these moments with Cisco. He was sure that his father would let him pretend to shoot a real gun just like Cisco did. Over Jimmy's few years of life his love and admiration for Cisco grew. The trips to Cisco's tiny rancharito were always an adventure.

"Jaime," Cisco said, pronouncing the boy's name in Spanish, "that procesión stretched along the ocean road farther than you could see. It was magnifico. All the people and their animals looked like they were walking into the dust at the front end of the long parade and out of the dust at the far end."

With his left eye tightly closed, Jimmy struggled to hold the heavy gun out in shooting position. Lupito kept one worried ear turned back toward Jimmy as the boy held Cisco's gun.

"Were you scared of those Caquista-doors?" Jimmy quizzed Cisco with wide, curious eyes. The whole issue of the doors confused his young innocent mind.

"Course I was. Those were very dangerous times, Mijo." Cisco confessed. "You never knew what to expect. I hid behind tall round rocks, being very careful that the feather I wore on the back of my head couldn't be seen by the highway men."

Jimmy sat bouncing along on the wagon's bench considering Cisco's feather and amazed by his bravery. "Did you ever get caught by them?"

"One time I had to rescue a beautiful señorita imprisoned by the Padres. The mother superior at the convent in Mission San Francisco wanted her to become a Novicia Monja of the Sacred Heart. But Señorita Carolina had other plans. She struggled with the idea and rejected the sacrifice of sisterhood. She told me all this after I crept down to their camp and untied her hands. When the soldiers saw me, and the señorita untied, they came running. We were much faster than those clumsy old men wearing heavy leather and iron shirts and iron hats. We ran very far away and hid in the tall brush and bushes far from the trail. With the help of the fog they never found us but I was very scared."

Cisco's memories and details amazed Jimmy. "Where did you go?" Jimmy continued.

"The señorita and I stayed very silent and crept south and inland away from the ocean for many days. We gathered seeds and berries and onions from the land to eat. We slept cuddled together for warmth in shelters we made from brush and straw. We whispered to each other instead of talking out loud."

"What happened to the señorita?" Jimmy cut in.

"After many days, we found the water hole near San Benito. With the clear clean water and soft moist dirt, it looked like a fine place to live. The beautiful señorita and I worked together building our cabin from straw and mud. She enjoyed stomping in the cool, wet adobe just like you and Lina. Sometimes to cool off on hot days, we wrestled in the cool pit and looked like muddy monsters. We cultivated the land around the water hole. We planted vegetables and fruit trees whenever we found seeds or roots. People started to know were we lived. Over time, from folks stopping by to say hello, the walk from Coaling Station A to San Benito became the main trail. Our love grew with the land. But God played a prank on us. Carolina died very young giving birth to our daughter Nela. I've lived a long life without the bonita señorita for a short time known as, Señora Carolina Francisco Hernandez, mi esposa. Nela and I have found happiness in the people moving into the west. And of course you know Oscar Saldoña, Nela's husband, a very hard-working man. They have their daughter, your friend, Lina, and their other children. And so we have lived happily by the adobe pit. Now you know the story of the beautiful Carolina and how I saved her from the Padres. But maybe God meant for her to stay with the Sacred Heart Sisters. So to get even with me he made her his angel, instead of mine."

Soon the compadres, Cisco, Lupito and Jimmy, rumbling along the gritty trail, arrived at Dust Creek.

Lupito possessed a typically mulish attitude. At the creek ford, he stopped and stared straight ahead over the shallow water, playing his part in a silly ritual of man versus beast. Jimmy felt sorry for Lupito. It seemed obvious how difficult it was for the mule to pull the heavy wagon over the rocks, through the water, up the soft muddy dirt, and back onto the road on the other side of the creek.

Cisco learned many years before that if he pulled his revolver and fired a shot into the sky he could get Lupito's attention. After a few training shots Cisco only had to shake the pistol over his head. The rattle of the cylinder and the sight of the potentially explosive weapon made Lupito squint his eyes, fold back his ears, turn his head, and bite at the harness. With no other alternative, the stubborn beast leaned forward with great effort and a humorous, grueling look on his oversized eyebrows. He trudged as slowly as he could, pulling the heavy cart into the water and across the creek. The looks on Jimmy and Cisco's faces mindlessly mimicked Lupito's. They glanced at one another then back at Lupito then back at one another. As they had many times before, they shook their heads from side to side, rolled their eyes and said, "Sheesh!" in unison.

At Cisco's cabin, Jimmy stood up in the wagon and jumped off running before the wagon had stopped. "Mijo don' jump like that. You coul' get hurt!" Cisco kindly scolded Jimmy.

"I'm sorry Cisco." The boy never wanted Cisco to be mad at him. He loved Cisco like a father. And he loved to make adobe bricks and stomp barefoot in the huge puddle of cool adobe mud and straw with all the brown eyed, brown haired grandchildren who called Cisco "Bapa"!

Lina, Cisco's oldest granddaughter, was the same age as Jimmy. She ran up to him and grabbed his hand. "Come on, Jimmy!" They ran off to jump into the refreshing, cool mud in the pit.

The number of finished bricks was negligible when the children "worked" in the adobe pit. The amount of fun and revelry far exceeded the amount of work actually done.

"Mijos, andale, ven aqui," Cisco called. And six, wet, muddy children, including Jimmy, came running. Lina took charge and lined up the children by height, the youngest going first.

"Gracias, Lina. You are very kind and have done a very good job of lining everybody up." One at a time Cisco gently stood them in the wooden half barrel of water warmed by the afternoon sun.

Tavo, first in line, wiggled and tried to escape. "Bapa! Stop it!" little Tavo hollered.

Cisco leaned his head very far back. With his most serious and humorous look he leaned Tavo precariously backward over the barrel. He peered down his nose at the side of Tavo's head for his overly precise inspection. Tavo cried with alligator tears and squirmed to get loose. Cisco pursed his lips and raised his eyebrows very high and said in his Doctor Bomba voice. "My goodness, Señor Gustavo! How did you get adobe mud so far down in your ears?" The other fidgeting children in line watched Tavo and Bapa intently as Cisco gently dug out the mud. They poked their tiny little fingers in their own ears checking if they had any mud. "This mud in your ears is of the best quality. You've done a very good job of mushing the adobe for your old friend, Dr. Bomba." The little boy giggled and wiggled and jumped from the tub running to escape from his bath. Lina grabbed him by the arm mid stride, swinging him out and back, as he attempted to run off.

"That's okay, Lina." Cisco said, "Señor Gustavo knows when he's clean enough. I hope no potato bugs grow in his ears to eat his brains out."

The rest of the tiny gang laughed at their grandfather. "Yaaa! The potato bugs are going to eat out Tavo's brains!" they cackled.

Tavo stomped and crossed his arms. Pouting and pressing his big head and chin firmly against his chest, "I don't have any brains for the potato bugs to eat!" he insisted.

The other children laughed even longer and louder.

Cisco, and his helper Lina, washed the rest of the children with an old rag. The brood turned from slippery brown to pinky orange. When they were ready to go into the cabin, from the haze of diluted pink/orange dry mud left on their skin, they looked like powdered debutante children from a French estate. Cisco knew the adobe powder kept insects and such from infesting his little monsters.

The three-room cabin was tidy and clean, except the

children's room which was wall-to-wall blankets, dolls, sticks, bird's nests, and from time to time, piglets, kid goats, puppies, or baby chicks. The cabin burst to life when the children swarmed in to investigate all the fascinating things they had collected during adventures romping around the ranch.

Three days later all the grandchildren were up early and excited. They had heard everyone talking about the one-hundredth birthday of the United States. The morning of the Fourth of July, 'el Cuatro de Julio,' prepared for the huge celebration, Jimmy rode back into town with Cisco and his friends in the wagon.

Loaded heavily with melons, potatoes, sweet corn, tamales and grandchildren the wagon lumbered up Cross Road and right at Main Street. Diagonally across the intersection Lupito stopped. The mule appeared once again to be in a trance. He stared into the shade as Cisco's buckboard rig blocked the busy road, forcing riders and pedestrians to detour around the wagon. Lupito ignored Cisco slapping his haunches with loose leather driving reins.

A few seconds later, Baxter Boreen, riding his tall black stallion named 'Maybe,' came up Dust Creek Road from the west. As he rounded the corner he saw Lupito in his trance and Cisco's wagon blocking his way.

"Cisco," Jimmy whispered and pointed off to the left.

"Si, Jaime?" Cisco whispered back.

“Baxter won’t like it if he has to go ‘round.” Jimmy warned.

Baxter was six feet three inches tall, with a tight, jet-black braid hanging straight down his back to his waist. Piercing blue eyes, and a long pointed nose with a bony hump halfway down from the top gave Baxter a hard angry look, even when he was happy.

Baxter generally avoided the town’s social events. The verdict of innuendo and gossip established that the citizens of San Benito were not fond of Baxter’s mysterious way of life. Nobody had ever seen him put in a day’s work. How could he always have money to gamble and drink? This was suspicious behavior to the hard working farmers who scratched a living out of the stingy, dry ground of San Benito.

At Cisco’s rig, ‘Maybe,’ the huge stallion, stopped abruptly, shied, and sidestepped quickly to the right, away from the farm wagon. “Whoa, Maybe!” Baxter roared. The sight and smell of the mule frightened the lawless horse. He squealed deep from his throat, arched his back, and tried to heave Baxter from the saddle. ‘Maybe’ repeatedly kicked his hind legs, throwing Baxter back and forth like a rag doll. But Baxter, the experienced buckaroo, dropped his heels, slouched in the saddle and planted the seat of his pants deep into ‘Maybe’s’ leather chair. He artfully followed the horse’s jarring bucks. Up and down they went until with one last leap the stallion settled in an uneasy, stiff legged stance in the street.

Not far away, Cisco lashed the driving reins again and

harder, desperate to get Lupito's attention and move the wagon away from Baxter's crazy horse.

"Andale, hombre!" Baxter barked at the old man, unintentionally jerking the reins back on 'Maybe's' sensitive mouth, "Move that heap of a rig!" The big, black stallion stepped quickly, going nowhere, dancing nervously in place. Suddenly, 'Maybe's' front hooves and fetlocks paddled high out in front. He reared dreadfully high on his hind legs. It was a long, bouncy, almost over-backward leap that frightened Baxter nearly to death.

"Si, Amigo. Momentito, por favor." Cisco grinned nervously to himself.

Not a patient man, Baxter didn't yield to anyone -- man, woman, or child. He was plain old rude, loud, big and vicious. Everybody felt a lot better when Baxter was not around.

Cisco panicked. Lupito sulked. Baxter's heart pounded atop the raging horse. 'Maybe' continued his dance stirring up clouds of dust floating above the dirt street. Passing pedestrians waved ineffectively at their faces attempting not to breath Baxter's dust.

Gathering the reins in his left fist he swatted at Lupito's rear. Then Cisco stood up in the wagon shouting at the dimwitted beast, "¡Andale, ahora mismo!" His worried breath burned in his chest. Then, without thinking, he pulled the revolver from his belt, a natural act for Cisco and Lupito, but a threatening gesture to Baxter.

“Mira aqui gringo! This mule won’t move! I’m trying to get him out of your way!” Cisco pleaded.

As Cisco shouted, and waved the pistol, he paid attention to Lupito. Baxter’s heart seized at the sight of Cisco’s gun. Jimmy watched Baxter and could tell by his ghastly expression that he didn’t know how Cisco had trained Lupito with the old revolver.

“No!” Jimmy screamed, lunging from the seat, waving his arms, “It’s for the . . .”

Cisco didn’t have a chance to make Lupito move the wagon. Baxter had grabbed his Colt forty-five pistol from the holster with his right hand and quickly pointed it across ‘Maybe’s’ tangled, sweaty, mane. From twenty feet away, Cisco looked up just as Baxter pointed the gun. Cisco’s kind old eyes met Baxter’s. In that moment Baxter knew Cisco intended him no harm and could have aborted his defense. But the hardened villain, obsessed with defending against constant oncoming trouble, with tangled reins in his left fist, fanned the gun hammer without thinking.

The bizarre sounds of the shots were eerily confusing. First the loud explosion from the gun, of course, immediately followed by the unexpected smack sound as the bullet hit Cisco’s flesh. Very quickly, the sound, “*Kablam blap, kablam blap!*” resounded as Baxter fired in rapid succession. It was not funny at all, horrifying to everyone nearby.

Flinching at the blast from the gun, and fighting

Baxter's oblivious jerks on the reins, 'Maybe', the stud horse, spun his left hip toward Cisco. Baxter's head turned to stay in line with the old man, as 'Maybe' spun. Baxter looked over his left shoulder when the two slugs of fire breathing lead exploded from his gun. The first grazed Jimmy's left shoulder knocking him out of the wagon, and then it pierced Cisco's heart. The second chunk of lead came to rest not an inch from the first, ending any hope for Cisco's survival.

The ringing in Jimmy's ears from the gunshots deafened him. The boy was mindless of his lifesaving attempt. With his hands behind him deep in the street's dust, he wavered as he sat up, "Ohhh Cisco," his high voice gasped, "Are you okay?"

Cisco didn't answer. His head didn't nod. His eyes didn't blink. The thought that Cisco would come up smiling, his eyes would pop open and twinkle and he would tell Jimmy that he was okay, that he was just joking, quickly passed. Cisco's pose looked comfortable, as though he were pleasantly asleep on the street; which in itself proclaimed the eerie truth of the matter.

Cisco's clouding eyes blindly stared at his hand that still held the simple, rusty gun. Dirt stirred by Cisco's hard landing, covered the end of the gun's barrel. Jimmy's eyes followed along Cisco's lifeless arm to the old .44 caliber, cap and ball, Dragoon.

Cisco's grandchildren who had ridden in with Jimmy and Cisco were crouched in the wagon. Peeking over the sideboards, befuddled at first, they quickly realized what had just happened. Their big, brown, teary eyes gaped wide in fear.

"Shhhh!" Lina whispered sternly to her brothers and sisters with an urgent, demanding voice, "Baxter might shoot again!" Her tiny, little fingers, and white knuckles, gripped the top sideboard tightly, in sheer panic and terror.

Then Jimmy looked up at Baxter through blurring tears, and snuffled, "Why?" The confused anguish in his young falsetto voice explained it all.

"Why?!" growled Baxter, insincerely, "Everyone here saw the old man pull his gun! -- 'n who 're you t' ask me why?" Forehead and eyebrows cross with furry, he towered against the sun-dried sky. Repugnant and overpowering, he spoke to the little boy, intending everyone nearby to hear his declaration.

Squatting in his tears, Jimmy sniveled courageously, "I'm Jimmy Longhon and Cisco was my best friend!" He choked on the oppressive words. His dead friend's life puddled in the street. The pungent odor of blood, intestines, and burnt gunpowder, lingered in the air, a memory unfit for a budding mind.

Baxter grinned nervously and mocked Jimmy's name, "Long Gun, that's a hell of a name, for such a little man." Baxter turned toward the group of curious gawkers. He surveyed for trouble as more men hustled up the street to see what the disturbance was.

A moment passed while Baxter turned away. Without

forethought or malice, Jimmy struggled quizzically to lift Cisco's cocked and loaded revolver. Its weight felt good in his hand, but the miserable excitement of the moment shamed any pleasant thoughts.

With an overconfident attitude, scowling eyes, intending to speak again, Baxter turned back to the boy.

Jimmy flinched from the gun's concussion. The weapon jumped in his hands. Strands of hair on his forehead puffed into the air as hot gas escaped from the worn, loose cylinder of Cisco's old farm implement of a gun. It wasn't clear to anyone close by, or to Jimmy for that matter, whether he pulled the trigger deliberately, or if the gun went off by accident.

Paralyzed from the impact of the bullet, Baxter dropped his revolver. His eyebrows arched. His mouth stretched wide, confounded by the pain. Clutching his traumatically bloody chest, Baxter stared into the youthful bright blue eyes and the soft innocent face of little Jimmy Longhon. Unable to speak clearly Baxter choked out the words, "You're just a child and you shot me dead in the chest. I'm very sorry boy." Then he leaned forward very slowly.

Jimmy looked back into Baxter's dying eyes. The respect of the now quiet, frightened man, unable to take back his mistake confused Jimmy. "You were so shameful and now you're so polite, I don't get it, Mr. Boreen."

Baxter finally fell from his horse and landed in a pile

on the dusty path to eternity. Along the road and beyond the town, the gunshot's echo faded into the distant silence following the thud of Baxter's limp body landing in the street. With words that no one could hear, except Jimmy, his face covered in blood, sweat, and dust, Baxter whispered blindly in Jimmy's direction. "Don't start 'n end your life the way I have." For an instant Jimmy pondered unshooting the gun -- obviously impossible.

Bewildered by the lighter load, with one ear searching over his back, a confused expression crossed 'Maybe's' face. Then he perked his ears forward nervously. Still keyed up, he briskly looked around. Flinching and quivering at every vibration, he leaned down, sniffed the fallen man, snorted with displeasure, and then took five quick steps backward. Finding no restraint on the reins he arched his back and loped off west, down the road that Baxter came in from.

Elsie Cutchel, four years old, stepped out onto the boardwalk from inside the store when she heard the shots. "Come back here!" Her mother quickly scooted out and grabbed her.

Elsie peeked around from behind her mother's dress, "Jimmy!" she shouted at the top of her little voice, but he was too far away. "I don't think he can hear me," she said looking up at her mother. "He never wants to play with me." Her looks of admiration toward the older little boy gave away her innocent affection for him. As on many other days, he was too busy to pay attention to her.

"You must understand how serious this is, Elsie! Jimmy is in a lot of trouble!" Her mother scolded, looking down crossly, and giving Elsie a shake.

After his mother bandaged his wound, Jimmy couldn't sleep. He thought of Cisco's death. Even though he didn't completely understand what death meant, he knew it was bad. He wondered what his long lost father would have done.

He knew Cisco wasn't coming back and felt it was his fault. *"What did I do?"* His thoughts kept repeating. *"Maybe if I hadn't jumped and shouted Baxter wouldn't have fired his gun."*

The bullet that grazed him hadn't cut into muscle. The throbbing wound burned painfully. It felt as if the slug had ripped his arm completely off.

His mother continued to scold little Jimmy in the most loving way she could. Cuddling him in her arms and rocking him gently she said, "You had no business touchin' Cisco's gun." She admonished the boy. "My gosh, you could have been killt'!"

After she tucked him into his bed she tried to be quiet but continued to ramble, thinking Jimmy wasn't listening. "We aren't the kind of people t' go around shootin' uthus!"

From deep inside Jimmy's mind his father's words came to him. *"Dory, let the boy lick his wounds; this ain't no time to ride hard on him."* Jimmy was sure his father would have known the pain and guilt that he was feeling.

"Oh my." Dora whispered at the ceiling, missing her husband that she had loved so dearly, "Buck, I don't want trouble with folks around town. What 're they goin' to think of us now?" She worried aloud, humiliated. "I wish you were here. Just think of 'r reputation, and Jimmy's such a little guy?"

Jimmy wondered if his mother heard his father's voice as she spoke. The same voice he felt inside but could barely remember. *"Everyone around San Benito knew Jimmy wasn't trouble, and everyone around San Benito cared for the boy. Everyone around San Benito loved old Cisco. Baxter shouldn't have been so quick to shoot."*

Sad and weary, Jimmy tried to understand everything that happened that day but couldn't. He longed for his father to walk in the house and into his room at that moment and tell him that everything would be okay. But he knew he wouldn't.

He felt lonely and sorry for himself and was already missing Cisco. He felt a slight glow of satisfaction, muddled with guilt and shame. He wasn't looking forward to seeing any of his friends around town.

Jimmy actually understood as much as anybody else in town about what took place that day. He just wasn't old enough to know what he knew.

The next morning, the town's people buried Cisco and Baxter. Jimmy felt tired and sick to his stomach. His shoulder throbbed. He skulked alone through the high grass up to the crest of the hill overlooking the cemetery. His blond hair was barely visible along the tops of the sea of barley stocks as he tunneled through them. He sat in the tall weeds sucking a green barley stem. He silently watched for a very long time. Men finished filling in the graves and Cisco's friends and family had all left.

A chilly breeze swept over the vacant cemetery. Threatening clouds rolled along the horizon and the sky darkened. Through tears and blurry eyes, Jimmy glanced up from his lookout on the hill. In disbelief, he glanced at the sky again, and then looked again intently. He thought he saw three men on horseback, riding away from the cemetery, into the eternal sky. Maybe they were just clouds.

Sadness gripped his eyes and throat. He walked down the hill and through the rickety, Iron Gate attached to the ornate picket fence that enclosed the cemetery. Unable to sort out the horrible events, he made up his mind to not think about that day ever again.

"I'm sorry Cisco. I didn't mean to g't you kil't." Jimmy blubbered, standing quite close looking down over Cisco's freshly mounded grave. He crouched down and scooped up a handful of the dirt. From somwhere else in time or space holding the dirt had a grounding effect on the boy, sucked the hurt right out of him. His heart felt calm with a refreshed strength and energy that lifted the boy's spirit, opening his eyes to a calm renewed morality.

Aside from that, Baxter Boreen's bony skull still holds the villain's wild expression of shock and bewilderment, from the day of consequence, when little Jimmy Longhon shot him in the chest, stopping his black heart cold.

Chapter Two
1883

Gossip about the 'Cuatro de Julio of '76' lasted a very long time. To some, Jimmy was, "a good kid, seein' that nobody had a nice thing to say about Baxter." Others thought he was bad and one to be avoided. "Involved in gun play and not even six years old." Bad or good, the reputation was his. It tagged along close behind him for the rest of his life. Beginning that day of consequence in July, his existence appeared to be directed by an unseen force. It had the power of a tidal wave. It picked Jimmy up by the shoulders and shoved him along, at times, so fast he could barely keep up without tripping over his own feet without a father to prop him up.

At first, the years passed slowly. Jimmy kept more to himself. But he was still more respectful to his elders than most of the kids around town. He tipped his hat to his mother's friends and other women he came across in the little town -- when he remembered.

Jimmy didn't say a lot when he went out in public. Some people figured the shooting twisted his mind. He didn't think about it much, just felt shy around people. Then a month or a year would go by and to his shame he would overhear some stranger getting filled in.

The other kids rarely bothered him about it. They

would fish and swim in the reservoir on hot Sunday afternoons as if nothing had ever happened.

With chores, school, and church, he didn't have time for trouble, but sometimes, it just seemed to find him. In a box of nails and screws and other lost metal widgets his father had left in the barn years before, he found a thirty-two-caliber rim fire rifle cartridge. Its uncommon size and shape intrigued him. His buddy Aaron owned a single shot rifle that the boys agreed, "it might just fit." One Saturday, sitting in Aaron's room, Jimmy pulled the cartridge out of his pocket.

"Let's see if she's a match." Aaron suggested, taking the peculiar looking trinket from Jimmy's hand. He took the rifle off the rack, bent it open and inserted the cartridge. "Yep. I never thought this ol' rifle had bullets to fit it anymore." Then absentmindedly put the rifle back on the gun rack still loaded and cocked.

A few minutes later with renewed interest, forgetting that it was loaded Jimmy took the rifle back down. "I bet this would be a nice gun for those big ol' raccoons, hidin' up in the corn crib."

"Ya. That would get 'em down f'r sure." Aaron replied, leaning by his bedroom window.

Thoughtlessly, the gun lying across his knees, Jimmy fiddled with the trigger. The hammer fell. The rifle leapt and blasted an earsplitting peel. A neat hole appeared in the wooden siding covering the inside of the room.

The boys tossed the rifle on the bed and ran to assess the

damage. They found that the bullet had smashed through the bedroom wall. It had crossed the hall, and had pierced another clean hole through the far wall. Then it hit and shattered a four-by-four-inch post inside the cabinet.

With their eyes wide and round, brows high and slack jawed, Aaron and Jimmy looked at one another like owls.

"Gosh Aaron, I would o' thought that bullet would be stuck deep into that four by four after all that, but it's just lyin' here on the shelf." Jimmy pointed out.

Needless to say, Aaron's parents scolded the two boys thoroughly. "What were you thinking?" Aaron's father pressed. "You're both twelve years old and I know you know better than to load and cock a gun in the house! You could have killed your little sister!"

Jimmy's mother repeated the lecture and then some. Aaron's father, Fred Hochberg, and Dora Longhon chose a fitting punishment for the boys' foolishness. "To keep you out of any more trouble this summer you boys can dig a ditch from the Hochberg's pig yard to the lower field to drain slurry from the pen." Mrs. Longhon told the boys, as they stood slightly slouched at attention.

With looks of despair sagging on their faces Jimmy whispered to Aaron, "It wouldn't be so bad if the summer hadn't already dried that ground to a crispy, gravely, solid cake. That ground 'ill be hard to break with a pick, and impossible with a shovel."

"If it was spring, it would be easy," Aaron added.

One hot day as the boys struggled with their ditch, Elsie rode to the store in the buckboard with her mother. She smiled at her dusty, sweaty friends. "Hey Jimmy," she smiled as they lumbered by.

Jimmy smiled back in silence, contemplating his dirty appearance, slightly embarrassed that he wasn't wearing a shirt.

Elsie noticed the boy's sweaty faces and muscular, shirt-less torsoes. She even felt a shortness of breath and leap in her heartbeat that she had never noticed before.

After shopping, Elsie stepped out of the store before her mother, the same way she did, years before, on Jimmy's dreadful day. She stood fiddling with the dime her father had given her when Little Walt walked up. She accidentally dropped the dime and it rolled off below the boardwalk into a small shaded mud puddle, still waiting to dry up, from spring. The dime made a perfect shiny circle against the brown mire, too far to reach from the raised wooden walkway.

Walt saw Elsie and her dime and jumped right after it into the mucky puddle. Not feeling like an insider in San Benito, he was always trying to impress the other kids around town. "Finder's keepers." He proclaimed brightly, not giving a thought to his muddy pants or shoes.

"Give it back, Walt, my pa gave it to me." Elsie insisted.

Originally hoping to endear Elsie, Walt had every

intention of giving the dime back to her. But when she barked at him, he changed his mind and wouldn't budge. He continued to tease her, waving the small coin close to her face.

When Jimmy saw Elsie and the Cutchel's red mule moments before, he began looking to see where she went. Walt had worked Elsie into a fit. Her face was bright red as she prepared to dive in and tackle him right there in the mud by the water trough. Striding up the wooden planks, half naked, Jimmy heard what was going on. "Give it back to her Walt." Jimmy insisted.

Walt, a year older than Jimmy, two inches taller and about the same weight said, "Don't tell me what to do, Long Gun." Even he was awestruck by Jimmy's lean muscular frame, glistening in the sunlight.

Walt belligerently pushed Jimmy's shoulders, backing him up the boardwalk, and telling him off. "I heard about what you did to Aaron's bedroom wall. What a loser. Go back to digging ditches, Long Gun!" He repeated his insult.

Jimmy warily looked up at Walt. The older boy intimidated him. His heart pounded. Trembling, he couldn't catch his breath easily. Without a plan or even thinking about it, Jimmy snapped his left hand out and snatched the dime. He removed it from Walt's fingers so quickly, that Walt stood amazed and angered. With his right fist he punched Walt in the face. Closing the dime in his left fist he threw nine more quick punches. By the third strike Walt's nose began to bleed. The blood from his nose quickly turned Jimmy's fists bright red.

Worried that Walt might be seriously hurt; Jimmy stopped punching and leaned forward. "You okay?" he asked. While Jimmy leaned close, concerned for what he had done, Walt whirled suddenly and pasted him square in the eye. Jimmy leaned his shoulder against the wall of the general store. Walt cocked his arm back to hit Jimmy again, even though Jimmy was obviously out of the fight. As Walt came around mid-swing, Jimmy unexpectedly leaned down and forward, to cup his hands over his eyes. Walt couldn't stop the momentum of his strafe. With great force, fanning right over the top of Jimmy's head, he inadvertently slammed his fist into the wooden wall. Just in time Mrs. Cutchel stepped out to intervene.

"You two stop it right now! Do you hear me?" She hollered.

Marcy marched the two boys up to see Shorty. "I'm goin' to git your mother, Mr. Longhon. Good thing your parents are so far out or you'd be in more trouble too!" She said, pointing a serious finger at Little Walt.

Shorty was the town's blacksmith, quasi veterinarian, and, next to Lolo Fernandez, the barber, the closest thing around to a doctor. "You two boys is too young to be fightin' over this gal. Quit your brawlin, and marry her!" Shorty joked with knowitall undertones.

Elsie ducked her head and blushed at Shorty's humor. Jimmy shrugged, "I don't think so, Shorty."

Walt scowled with his head bent down, and didn't speak.

Jimmy grinned at Aaron and Elsie standing close together sheepishly avoiding any fallout scolding that might come their way.

Shorty checked Jimmy's eye. It was not working right at first. But after a little while, his pupil began to respond.

Walt's hand was not broken but it was very swollen. His nose would never be the same.

As the boys left the livery Walt walked up close in back of Jimmy, kicked Jimmy's left ankle over and behind his right calf and tripped him up, "Meet me behind the hotel after lunch. I'm going to finish this."

With his threat Little Walt was through. He saddled up his horse and rode east out of town toward home.

Jimmy hadn't seen Little Walt ride off. He walked and worried and clenched tighter on the dime still in his left hand. He figured he was just lucky, getting the punches in on Walt that he had. Down inside him something told Jimmy he had to show up. *"It's a responsibility or somethin',"* he said to himself.

At half past one, he headed for the hotel. He arrived to find all the kids in town gathered and waiting. At two o'clock Walt still wasn't there. The kids sat along the boardwalk kicking their feet just above the cracked, caked mud. Aaron spoke up, "That coward ain't coming back all that way from home."

"That Walt is just a big chicken turd," the others gossiped.

All of his young life, Jimmy had an affinity for people, always thinking the best of them. Talking dirt was never his way even if he didn't really like them.

"He ain't so bad," Jimmy said in a kindly manner, feeling sorry for Walt. "Maybe he's a little skinny t' go 'round shoving on people."

Jimmy's eye had turned into a huge purple shiner. "Here Elsie, I've got somethin' for you."

"The dime! How did you get it?" She giggled.

In the creases and crevasses, Walt's blood still stained the coin.

"Ahh, it weren't nothin', I just curt'osly, carefully and politely snatched it up right out of Little Walt's gentle hands." Jimmy smiled.

"Oh Jimmy, your eye, let me have a look." She stood up straight, with her shoulders back, in her best motherly stance. She stretched out her hands to hold Jimmy's head and assess his swollen eye.

"Ah, come on now. I don't want you lookin' at it. It's ugly and 'mbarrasses me." He turned away, feeling out of sorts.

All winter Jimmy and Aaron were inseparable and somehow found more innocent mischief to get into just like the rest of the preteen boys in San Benito. The following spring they turned thirteen.

After worrying about it in great detail, his mother decided to send Jimmy to stay with her sister, Mary Picket, in Stockton.

Dora Longhon thought her younger sister Mary was lonely and Jimmy could keep her company. He could help her with chores around the house, and maybe stay away from Aaron and monkey business for the summer.

Aunt Mary's husband had worked for the railroad. Until one sad day, four years before, he was standing on the tracks between two cars greasing the coupling. The train lurched without warning. The life was crushed out of him as the coupling pinned him to the other car.

Stockton, a ten-day trip on horse back, only took the better part of a day by train. Dora Longhon had absolutely no wherewithal to take Jimmy to Stockton herself. "Marcy I was wonderin' if you and Elsie could ride along with me when I take Jimmy to the train depot next Wednesday." Dora asked Marcy Cutchel coming out of church. "I wrote my sister Mary and she's expecting him Wednesday afternoon."

"I wish I could, Dora, but I told Nela I'd help her put up cabbage. They're goin' t' be just right next week."

Overhearing the two ladies Lolo the barber spoke up. "Puedo mees Dora. I c'n take Jeemy. I need de treep out o' town for a change. I coul' look aroun' an' ge' ou'ta town for a while."

"My my. That is so kind of you Lolo." Dora smiled in relief.

Before Jimmy could board the train there was a ten-mile ride to the depot at Coaling Station-A.

About two hours before sun up, Jimmy's mother grabbed him by the toe. "Wake up Jimmy, you've got a long day ahead of you."

"Okay, I'm comin'." He yawned.

Dora Longhon fried venison sausage and pancakes by kerosine lantern light under the porch awning in back of their house. Lolo and Shorty strolled into the yard in the early black morning, right on time and ready for breakfast. Jimmy harnessed up the horses. Shorty watched patiently as the boy threaded the reins and checked the button knots that held the gear in place. "Snaps and metal fittings are hard to find out here, them braided leather and rawhide buttons you got there work great instead of metal a lot of the time." Shorty unnecessarily informed Jimmy.

All hitched, the team stood quiet. Jimmy tossed his bag into the buckboard.

Jimmy's mom looked as cheery as she could. "Oh my." She whispered. She hugged his face against her bosom. He felt he was too old for so much hugging by his mom, especially with Shorty and Lolo watching. "Pay attention while you're traveling,

Jimmy. Be careful talking to strangers. Give your Aunt a hug and tell her I miss her."

The trip was his mother's idea, but now nagging thoughts pulled at her heart. She had never been away from her son before this, and felt troubled about him leaving. Lolo climbed into the buckboard and tucked the Longhon's single shot ten-gauge under the seat. With a yip and a thwack of the reins, the team leaned into their collars. The wagon rolled away.

At the last minute as a second thought, Shorty swung up next to Jimmy, "Ah heck, I might as well go along."

"Mind your Aunt!" His mother lifted her voice. She waved and held back her tears until the men were well out of sight. "Oh my goodness." She whispered to herself in her sweet southern accent.

As they bumped along, Shorty tried not to lecture but couldn't help himself. "Your ma's going to miss your help with the chores around there when you're gone. I hope your Aunt will 'preciate your visit and the help you c'n give her around the house."

"I know." Jimmy said quietly and nodded his head.

"D'you finish fixin' the plow harness, so's Lolo c'n turn over your ma's tater garden?"

"Yes-sir, she's ready to go" Jimmy mumbled.

"You behave yourself in Stockton. Mind your Aunt and stay out of fights."

"Yes-sir." Jimmy said again. *He didn't need to tell me that stuff.* He thought to himself. "I'll mind my manners and obey Aunt Mary." He promised.

After the five-hour, ten-mile ride, they rolled up to the hitching rail along side the train station, opposite the tracks. They stood up in the wagon stretching their backs and jumped down, grateful to be standing after such a long ride. Jimmy tethered the horses to the rail.

The depot, a small wooden building along the long steel track, had a low roof. The shingles and siding had weathered to gray. Cattlemen in the area drove their herds to this station. A raised wooden walk skirted around the outside for boarding the train. With all the pens and ramps along the siding, the station appeared to be built more for the ease of loading livestock and less for the comfort of the two-legged passengers.

Inside the train station there was a little more luxury, if it could be called that. At one end, inside the single room, stood a bar. At the other end of the room a telegraph key rested on the ticket desk. The clump of boot-heels echoed in the quiet room.

According to the code of the west, polite women didn't sit at a bar or in a saloon. That could invite trouble. In the middle of the room, there were tables and chairs encircling a pot bellied stove. These were for women and children to sit in while waiting for the train or incoming passengers. A checkerboard had a permanent spot on the table closest to the stove. If one was not there to eat or drink, time could be whittled away playing checkers with Whitey, the station clerk. A lot of time was used up, in that manner.

High on a sturdy, crisscrossed timber platform, outside the low, one-room building, and close to the tracks, stood a cylinder shaped, wooden water tank with large, white letters spelling COALING-A. A windmill next to the platform continually pumped water, keeping the tank full and ready to refill the boilers of the regularly arriving steam driven trains. The ground around the structure was damp from the leaks and splashes that occurred while filling the trains. Consequently, on this spot grew the only permanently green grass for miles around. A horse trough and hitching rail rested below the tank.

Dora Longhon had given Jimmy money to pay for the train fare and a little extra traveling money. The silver dollars were heavy and the twenty dollar gold piece was small and light and yet worth so much more. This quandary gave his young mind something to think about. The silver dollars felt good in his hand. Their weight reminded him of Cisco's revolver.

"Mornin' Mr. Whitmore" Jimmy said respectfully.

"Mornin' Jimmy, mornin' Lolo, Shorty."

"Mornin' Whitey." The pair coughed their respect. Oddly they treated Whitey as the local constable, even though he wasn't.

'Whitey Whitmore, the station keeper, was a man

with many hats. He usually had pots of stew and coffee going, which made him the cook. He responded to any incoming telegraph messages, which came in about twice a week. Just as often, some cowboy or lost soul would show up to send a telegram. That made him a telegrapher. He was the head ticket agent and railroad representative for the county. He ran the bar -- that made his life very risky. Drunken cowboys tended to punch and shoot first, rarely, if ever, giving any forewarning of their shenanigans. No matter how many hats he wore, his job was still very slow and sometimes very lonely.

Jimmy walked over to the desk where the telegraph key sat. “Mr Whitmore, I need a ticket to Stockton.”

“Round trip or one way?” Whitey asked facetiously, knowing very well the boy was going to visit his Aunt.

“I’ll be comin’ back in six weeks,” Jimmy told him.

“Then it’ll be cheaper to buy both tickets now.”

So that’s what Jimmy did. Lolo and Shorty grinned watching how the boy handled the little decision. “Well Jimmy, your ma won’t have to worry ‘bout you out there on this trip,” Shorty said profoundly.

Outside in the distance, the train whistle blew. Nobody else was in the station. Jimmy and the boys stepped out into the bright morning, and looked down the tracks. As they squinted off toward the horizon, a shot of steam rushed into the sky, and a few seconds later they heard the whistle.

"Isn't that funny how the steam starts and after a bit you hear the whistle?" Jimmy said.

"Sure is," Shorty tucked his thumbs in his sleeveless vest and leaned back with authority. "The sound waves move along slower than the light r'fectin' from the steam. So's ya see's there's this time misalignment deal." Lolo looked at Shorty, exhausted by the little sentence and shook his head in antipathy.

This unusual metaphysical event gave Jimmy a mysterious feeling about the quiet, sunny day.

Leaving his mother behind made Jimmy nervous and excited. He had never been away from her, except for hunting and camping trips, that were just overnighters.

The train, with only two passenger cars, slowly rolled up to the depot. The conductor leaned out of one of the car doors while the train was still rolling, tossed a leather bag down onto the platform and yelled, "Borrrrrt!"

Whitey, Lolo, and Shorty, walked with Jimmy to the car where the conductor was standing in the doorway. Jimmy handed the conductor his ticket.

"The boy 's travelin' t' Stockton t' visit his Aunt, Mary Picket. She'll be there this afternoon t' meet him." Shorty formally reported to the conductor.

"I'll be sure he gets safely into her arms." The black skinned man teased and winked at Jimmy.

Embarrassed, Jimmy wrinkled his eyebrows, and looked at his feet. "I'm not a baby."

Lolo ruffled his hair. "Hasta la vista Jaime. 'Member what your mo'r tol' you."

"I will." He mumbled.

Timidly, he stepped onto the massive train. It's futuristic appearance impressed and amazed him.

Jimmy saw only one other person, already in the train car. He seemed very old. His skin had very deep wrinkles that reminded him of old Polly, years ago. His deep, gray-blue eyes sparkled and he smiled at Jimmy as he stepped into sight.

San Benito was a very small town far away from the highways. Jimmy didn't meet strangers often, and he felt embarrassed. His manners were awkward. The old man stuck out his hand and said, "Howdy. I'm Russ Tanner. What do they call you?"

Bowled over by the cantankerous stranger, "Jimmy," he said shyly. Jimmy wasn't used to meeting new people and wasn't sure what to say or do. Jimmy quickly found out that Russ was an acquired taste, even for those with far more experience in life than this fledgling young traveler.

"Where ya' headed, son?" Russ pressed.

Jimmy felt uncomfortable to divulge his personal information but didn't have the tenacity to decline, "I'm going to visit my Aunt in Stockton." And maybe his youthful inexperience left him open to far more possibilities in the big scheme of things.

"Where's y'r ma and pa?"

Jimmy was very embarrassed and distrusting of the old man. But once again felt compelled to respond. If nothing else, out of respect, "My ma live's in San Benito. My pa lit out for Knoxville, Tennessee, in 1872, when I was just three years old. I barely 'member what he looks like. I think 'bout him every now n' then, wonder what he's doin', if he thinks about me. I don't think he does. Ma said he wanted to name me Sue! Can you believe that!?"

"Well, isn't that just the sadist thing I have ever heard," the old codger tried to console this young man he just met out of the blue. "You and your ma all alone in the middle of the far west. Why don't ya pack up and head out to Knoxville to find him?"

"I don't know. My ma never said nothin' like that."

"How long you stayin' up there in Stockton?" Russ continued with what seemed like an inquisition to Jimmy.

"Just a few weeks 'till school starts again, after summer."

Unable to sit quiet, Russ went on, "Born nearby Coaling Station A, were you?

"About ten miles west in San Benito, we have a little house in the middle of town." Jimmy answered. He was still very weary of the old Man. "My ma told me to be careful who I talked to on this trip." Jimmy stated, to clarify that he was in control of things.

"Whad'ja say your last name was?" Russ went on.

Jimmy didn't say. He just looked out the window at the bright arid landscape.

"I'll bet you I can guess." Russ pushed again.

Jimmy still didn't reply. He squirmed uncomfortably in his seat as the train rumbled along.

"I'll bet you your last name that you can't grab this penny out of my hand" Russ went on.

Jimmy thought old Russ was getting ridiculous with his interrogation. But he was intrigued by Russ's test. Grinning confidently, Jimmy took a swipe at the penny but Russ closed his fist far to fast for the boy to catch the penny.

"Ha haaa!" Old Russ laughed. "So tell me."

"Longhon." Jimmy whispered. He'd heard the jokes again and again and was almost prepared for Russ's reply.

"Did you say Long Gun -- that's quite a name for such a little hombre."

"Ya ya." Jimmy said insolently and embarrassed. He

rolled his eyes, and looked away out the window again.

Ever kill anyone?" Russ piped on teasingly.

Jimmy wasn't expecting that. And didn't know what to say. Jimmy's heart sank as he recalled the dreadful morning, eight years before.

Russ Tanner watched Jimmy's face turn from cautious wonder to a very sad thoughtful gaze. The old man didn't know what made the boy act so sad.

They both sat there in silence -- for a time that seemed uncomfortably long, so long that some might have called it a Texas minute. Jimmy fought back tears, thinking about the day Cisco died.

"Boy," Russ finally spoke, then paused and coughed quietly. "I'm awful sorry if anything I've said has made you mad. I didn't 'tend to make you quiet and sad. I 'tended on bringing up some conversation so's we could chit chat the day away like a couple of old hens, instead of bein' bored 'n' starin' out the window and ignorin' one 'nother. I set out on this trip to explorer America and it turns out traveling alone is far more borin' than I expected."

"Now you sit right there and listen up while I tell you why I'm so mad at the world and 'bout the first bandit I met in the wilds of Texas. This here fella' weren't a heck of a lot older than you. He probably'd only seen sixteen years of life, if that. He was full of himself. Want'n food or money, he rode up to a trading post 'bout seven miles outside Abilene. Right there in the blazin' afternoon sun, he pulls his iron and shoots the store keeper right smack between the eyes from five feet away. Made one huge mess I'll tell you. I seen the aftermath of it with my own eyes."

"Well, that ain't the worst of it. That trader was married to a wiry red haired gal from Ireland. She was ready to fix that crook's wagon with a Sharps buffalo rifle. He just reaches out and grabs the end of the barrel as she pulls the trigger. The shot scorched the skin from his wrist all the way up his left forearm. And the lead smashed out the stovepipe and made a big ol' hole in the wall. Then he bashes her upside the head with his pistol and she fell on the floor. 'Bout then he takes a shine to the purty little thang and decides she's goin' to be his darlin' right there on the trading post floor. The little gal opened her eyes and was ready to die b'fore bein' bred by that slimy murderer. The fight that ensued was a bad'n. When we found her she was bloody, bruised and unconscious. But she discouraged the boy from having his way with her."

"Our bandito headed for Abilene and to the first jolly house he could find. The madam took notice of his criminal-like appearance, scorched, scratched, and spattered with blood. She sent one of her gals to fetch the sheriff. I'd tracked the boy from the trading post and was sittin' in my saddle talkin' to the sheriff when the gal came runnin' up. The madam sent the boy to an empty room and the rest of the girls out the back door. The sheriff went in the front door and I went in the back. The boy must've heard the boot steps 'cause the varmint came runnin' out of that room lickety split, with his gun drawn; he stopped nose to nose with the sheriff and shot him in his shootin' shoulder. Then the boy ran to the back door. There I was. My pistol aimed high and tight, right on him. He raised his gun to shoot so I fired. It didn't hit him solid, just spun him around. His gun went off and the slug made a good graze on my right knee. It knocked me to the ground but I kept my gun pointed right at him. He started to point his gun down at me again. I told him not to do it. He didn't listen. I had to shoot again. This time it knocked him down. The boy was dead when he hit the clay. Scared and shaking with excruciating pain, I couldn't get up. Before I passed out I threw up my own guts."

Jimmy listened to Russ's story. Russ's bravery impressed him. He understood the fear and rage Russ felt facing the wild, young outlaw. "I think I know what you mean." Jimmy was thinking of the time he had been shot. "So why were you talking to the sheriff of Abilene? Were you a sheriff from another town?"

"No," Russ said, "I was a Texas Ranger. It seemed like exciting work at the time. The pay weren't nothin' to brag on but it kept me out of the poor house for a while. Then, after my knee was blown out, the rangers didn't want me anymore. Damn them. They figured five hundred dollars was all my knee was worth. I got better at walkin' but would never get back a life like I knew. Never had me another girl since then. They always noticed my limp when I walked. Believe me though, it was a tough row to hoe. Even then though, I was a lucky one. Most of the boys got stove up pretty bad, worse than me. I don't recommend a life of law enforcement to anyone."

The arid land rumbled by as the boy and the old man talked.

"Here!" Russ said all excited all over again and held out his hand, palm up, with the penny in it. "Try and grab that out of my hand."

Jimmy tried another time.

Gently and quickly Russ snapped his fist shut and when Jimmy's hand arrived it met a closed fist with bony old knuckles. Jimmy looked into Russ's eyes with a calm, curious grin then quickly grabbed at Russ's open palm thinking he'd outsmart the old Texas Ranger. He tried repeatedly but he couldn't get the penny.

"Here, I bet'ch ya can't keep it from me."

Jimmy put the penny in his hand and held it out with confidence and pride, thinking this was the easy part. His young hand looked pink and smooth compared to old Russ's. Before he could blink Russ swiped the penny from his hand and sat there grinning at him.

"Djeese!" Jimmy twitched in frustration. Jimmy thought back to the day he snatched the dime out of Little Walt's hand.

"Now quit your bellyachin' and just let me try 'er again."

He tried over and over but couldn't keep Russ from snatching the penny from his hand.

"You see that boy? That's how you handle a gun if you're going to wear one. If you ain't that quick and confident you better not wear one or you'll find yourself looking up out of a long square hole on boot hill through glazed over eyes."

"How'd ya get out here in California," Jimmy asked, a little more warmly and trusting as the day went on.

"Without much left 'n life I finally, after so many years of sitting in Abilene, got fed up with all the big talkin', smart actin', slow drawlin' Texan's and decided to take a look at the rest of the world. I hobbled to the bank and withdrew my five hundred dollars. Bought a train ticket to Denver. Then I choked stagecoach dust all the way into Albuquerque. I promise you, I will never travel by stagecoach ever again; even if I have to walk. In Albuquerque I caught the train into The Pueblo de Los Angeles. And from there, here I am headin' to San Francisco."

The day was hot. The old Texas Ranger fascinated Jimmy. Time after time during the trip Jimmy tried to grab the penny from old Russ's hand but he couldn't do it. "Hey Russ" Jimmy broke in, "Did you ever do any cowboyin', branding and such?"

"No Jimmy. I spent my few early days chasing banditos 'cross Texas, 'till my leg got shot all up. But I always thought someday I'd own a big herd of long horn cattle."

Jimmy wanted to tell Russ about the fourth of July in '76. He wanted to tell him that he'd been shot in the arm once. But he thought Russ would be disappointed in him and just couldn't address it. "How come you don't wear a gun now, Mr. Tanner?

"Too heavy. And you can call me Russ. I'm so polite and good at keepin' my mouth shut -- ain't nobody wants to fight with a gimpy little old man like me." Old Russ grinned.

"Ya know the land back there by Coaling Station A can be used for running cattle. Me and my friend Aaron talked about getting us some cows and keeping a herd of our own."

"Well when I git some money some day, I'd be honored to invest in your cattle company," Russ proclaimed and poked Jimmy on the knee with his bony old index finger, "but for now I'm rich but I'm broke. So don't go counting your chickens, or cattle, before they hatch!"

The two talked the day away and didn't notice the sweltering heat. Jimmy warmed up to old Russ. The old grouch was so funny they spent most of the day laughing. Russ had stories and thoughts on life Jimmy would have never imagined.

Jimmy's plight in life touched Russ's heart. The old gimpy bachelor never expected the warm feelings of concern and companionship to well up so strong for the child. But there they were.

As the day got late, Russ fell asleep. Jimmy opened

his one side of a saddlebag. It was the same old one he'd had as long as he could remember. He took out a pencil and paper, and began to write a letter to old Russ.

The conductor came along and told Jimmy that Stockton was just ahead. The train's whistle blew and Jimmy wondered if the people at the depot in Stockton saw the steam before they heard the whistle.

Russ stirred when the whistle blew. He knew it was time to say, adios. He liked the boy. Jimmy was easy going and listened in earnest to Russ's stories.

"Are you goin' t' remember everything I told you about gun slingin' and takin' care of yourself and your guns?" Russ asked.

"Yes sir," Jimmy replied standing at attention looking deep into old Russ's eyes. "I won't ever misuse a gun as long as I live, Sir."

"Okay then, you and me's pards for life. Right?"

"You mean it?" Jimmy squeaked.

"I do. I never say a word I don't mean and expect the same. So's we pards or not?" Russ demanded. Then he lifted his hand toward his face and spit right into his palm. Then he stuck his sinewy claw out to Jimmy.

Disgusted at first, once again mystified by Russ's actions, with a puzzled expression, Jimmy looked down at Russ's hand then deep into his old wrinkled eyes. He hesitated for a moment. With a half serious look in his eyes Russ twitched his old hand toward Jimmy. Then with a big smile Jimmy spit into his own little pink hand, reached out and grabbed Russ's big old claw, "Yes sir! Pards for life!"

Jimmy was sad to say good-by to the old Texas Ranger, but too excited to show it. Had he been invited he might have gone on to San Francisco with Russ. Of course that would have started a whole new set of problems. So they made their good-byes. Just before he stepped off the train, Jimmy handed Russ his letter.

Chapter Three

Russ stood close behind Jimmy, with his hand on his shoulder, as the boy went down the train's steps. Russ beamed kindly and respectfully at Mary as she walked up to Jimmy, smiling. The hissing of the locomotive idling and rumbling made it impossible to say anything. Jimmy and his Aunt hadn't seen each other in many months, since the last time Mary came to San Benito to visit. "You've grown a mile, Jimmy," she said, giving him a tight hug that made him feel a little uncomfortable. "It's just fine to see you! Who was that man you were talking to on the train?" Mary had a similar southern accent, a little more sing song, than Jimmy's mother.

Jimmy was still thinking about Russ, but he was glad to see his aunt. "It's good seein' you too Aunt Mary. That old guy on the train there, he's my new pard, Russ Tanner. He's a retired Texas Ranger. He's going to invest money in me 'n Arron's cattle company."

Having traveled all day alone, Jimmy felt empowered. He was excited and proud. "Russ is going to San Francisco cause he's never been there before." He told his Aunt.

The town of Stockton seemed to bustle compared to San Benito. The strong summer sun reflected warm and bright off the dusty road.

The day of travel and adventure had stirred Jimmy's lust for life. Russ's kindness and interest in him made him feel unique and good about himself. He couldn't stop thinking of how quick the old ranger snatched the pennies from his hand. Jimmy held out an Indian-head cent and said, "Here Aunt Mary, try and grab this penny out of my hand."

She looked at him inquisitively and with very little effort, snatched the penny away. "Okay?" she asked.

Jimmy curled his lips and face, as he'd been known to do. He thought he would snap his fist shut and then tell her if she was not that sure and confident, she had better not handle guns. Now he wasn't sure if Russ had done it well because Jimmy was young and slow, or if his aunt was very quick. It almost ruined his day. Except the excitement about his trip and making friends with Russ hadn't worn off yet. He bounced right back.

Jimmy's Aunt worked in the office at the stockyards. She didn't need to work. Her husband was part of the first group of men, that started in eighteen seventy-four, to receive a pension from the railroad. That was enough money for her to live on. She worked to keep her mind active learning the cattle business. She had learned how the buyers and middlemen made thousands of dollars, just by adding as little as a quarter cent per pound to the price of the cattle. If some drover came in with five hundred steers, each weighing around nine hundred pounds, the whole herd would weigh about four hundred and fifty thousand pounds. Multiply that by a quarter cent, and it equaled over a thousand dollars, just for knowing who to telegraph in San Francisco.

As Jimmy and his aunt walked up the street, they passed the gunsmith's shop. "Can we go in and look at the pistols Aunt Mary? I really want to buy one so I can be just like Russ."

His Aunt knew about the lust for guns that young boys were born with. She knew that on the western frontier, guns were a part of everyday life, especially life farther out from the cities. She also knew about Cisco, Baxter and "the shooting in seventy-six" and felt a pang of apprehension. "Okay, just for a little bit."

Harley "Potwolloper" Rand, who owned the gun-shop, was a crack shot, and the best gunsmith in Stockton. His friends called him Pots. He earned the name as a boy by hanging one of his mother's cast iron skillets in a tree and hitting it dead center, five out of six shots at fifty paces. He never got a chance to make the sixth shot. Pots' old mother came out to see what the gunfire and clanging was all about. It was a good thing she wasn't armed or Pots might not have lived to get the name Potwolloper so well established.

"Howdy, Mary. Howdy, Boy, I'm Pots. What's your name?" Pots noticed right off and shared the boy's fascination with the guns. "Fixin' to do some shootin'?"

"This is my nephew, Jimmy." Mary told the cheery proprietor.

"I'm gonna learn everything there is to know about guns and shootin'." Jimmy told Pots. "I'm gonna to do it right and be the best shot there is."

"Where 'ya goin'ta get the money? I could teach you but cartridges ain't cheap and the only way to get good at shootin', is by shootin'."

"I've got a little traveling money my ma gave me. I could take four bits of it and buy a box of cartridges for practice. Do you think that would be okay, Aunt Mary?"

"I'm sorry Jimmy, but I don't think your mom sent you here with that money to buy bullets." She knew Pots' reputation for safety and precision. In fact Shorty and Lolo, clear down in San Benito, talked about Harley Rand's championship shooting. But Jimmy's Aunt also knew about Jimmy's calamity on the fourth of July in seventy-six.

"But, Aunt Mary!" Jimmy complained. "It's my money. Can't you see that I need to learn to shoot?"

"I know, honey. We'll talk about it at home. Good night, Pots. Thanks for showing Jimmy your store."

"G'night Mary, night Jimmy. Stop in anytime."

Jimmy and Aunt Mary walked on home. Jimmy continued his explanation on why he should learn to shoot. Jimmy's mind was swimming with excitement but deeply disappointed in his Aunt's dissent about him shooting with Pots.

On the other hand, he thought about how this morning his ma had been fixing him breakfast in the dark. Now here he was in Stockton with two new friends.

Chapter Four

After Jimmy left the train, Russ sat down and unfolded Jimmy's letter.

Dear Mr. Tanner, I just couldn't tell you before, but when I was five, Baxter Boreen shot my friend Cisco and killed him. I even got shot too. I was sitting next to Cisco's pistol. So, I just picked it up and shot Baxter back -- he died, but I really didn't mean for him to die. I really liked meeting you today. I hope you have fun in San Francisco. And I promise never ever to fool around with guns, like you said. If you ever come by Coaling Station-A or San Benito, I hope you'll come and see me and meet my mom and maybe my dad when he comes back from Tennessee. Your Friend, James Longhon.

"Well I'll be damned. I heard about that," Russ thought out loud. He folded up Jimmy's letter and tucked it in his breast pocket.

Russ, being Russ, drummed up a conversation with Jack Gelman the next passenger that boarded the train in Stockton. Jack, a self-proclaimed professional gambler, told Russ about his system for winning at roulette. The problem was that Russ couldn't remember if he was supposed to wait for the same color, black or red, on the roulette wheel, to come up four times or eight times in a row.

When Russ arrived in San Francisco, he went by trolley to the Palace Hotel. They had everything an old Texas Ranger could want: gambling, drinking and beautiful women.

Russ limped straight to the roulette table and sat down. After spinning the wheel three times, the croupier said, "I'm sorry, sir. You can't sit there unless you're going to place a bet."

"I'm goin, t', bet. I'm just waitin', for the raht time. And my knee is hurtin' me real bad."

"I'm sorry; you'll have to place a bet or stand up." The clerk insisted.

This put Russ in a terrible disposition. Impatiently, he stood watching the game. After what seemed like hours, the roulette ball landed on red four times in a row. So Russ placed a one-dollar bet on the black. Sure enough the ball landed on the black, which amazed Russ. With his L-shaped stick, the wheel's attendant pushed two one-dollar chips back at the amazed, and happily relieved winner. Russ waited for another long time. Every time the ball landed on the same color three times in a row he clenched his fists. Out of sheer will power, the ball should have landed on the same color but didn't.

Finally, the black came up a fourth time in a row. Thinking hard about it, with sweaty palms and heart pounding, he placed his five hundred dollars, everything he had, on red. As the wheel went around, he scrutinized it with serious anxiety. The thought of loosing his five hundred dollars brought out an extreme case of his undiagnosed disorder, non compos mentis. No, he was not really going crazy. But the other players around him definitely thought so.

As the wheel slowed, the ball clattered from number to number, black to red to black and so on. Russ stood fidgeting with anticipation. The little white ball finally settled down onto the number thirty-two -- red. "What a relief!" He fussed. The apprehension of whether he would win or loose drove him to his wits end. But winning mesmerized him. It was too easy. He couldn't understand why everyone didn't do this for a living. He didn't realize how much luck he had just fallen into. Had he lost, the outcome would have been equally dramatic, if not more.

The next day, walking on Market Street, Russ saw Jack Gelman coming out of a pawnshop. Jack was standing outside of the window when Russ strolled up. "Howdy Jack, I guess y'r sitting pretty if you had the same luck I had last night."

"I lost my money, all my money!" Jack repeated.

"What dja mean hombre?" Russ was puzzled.

"I know, I know…" Jack went on.

"But Jack, your system worked perfectly. I waited for the same color to come up four times in a row just like you said. Then I bet…"

"It isn't four times!" Jack contended. "It's eight times! You have to wait for the color to come up eight times then you bet the other color. Then the odds are one in three hundred of the same color coming up again!" Jack asserted hysterically.

"So the way I used your system was all wrong?" Russ tried to understand. "But I won over ten thousand dollars!" Russ rejoiced. "What about your system."

"I thought I had one. I waited and waited. The red finally came up eight times in a row. But I still lost." Sadly for Jack, who waited in front of the roulette wheel far longer than Russ, placed his one hundred dollar bet on black. But the ball, for the ninth time, found the red pocket once again. His heart sank like the iron clad USS Monitor off Cape Hatteras in 1863.

The back up plan, if Jack's system failed to produce a win, was to double his bet on the next spin of the wheel. And he did, two hundred dollars, two months pay. And once again he lost his money. The croupier hooked his cash, pulled it away, and stuffed it in a slot in the table. His heart, already on the bottom of the ocean, was now deep in a mire of despair. Terrified, but feeling no other choice, he put four hundred dollars, the last of his booty, once again on black. "It has to come up black this time," he said apprehensive of his own words.

The mob of anxious gamblers, around the table, who were following Jack's thinking to their own demise, piled their money up on top of Jacks. The pile of cash and chips was mind-boggling. But no, the red was the winner again. A chorus of displeasure moaned from the crowd. Jacks stomach began to churn. He felt nauseated standing at the table unable to double his bet again. The next spin of the wheel came up zero and then eighteen more times the ball landed on red. If Jack had continued doubling his bet he would have had $104,857,600.00 out on the table, probably a little over the table limit, to win back his original bet of one hundred dollars.

Jack was numb and broke and suicidal at his bad night of gambling. He returned to his room, and racked his brain, to find a solution to his financial ruin. He lay awake all night, rose early and walked out hoping something would occur to him. That's when Russ happened along.

"I don't know what I'm goin' t' do." He moaned. "I don't know how I'm goin' to pay my hotel room. Do you want to buy this gold watch?"

"I'm sorry Jack." Russ said hoping to settle him down. "I couldn't remember. I thought it was four." Russ reached into his pocket and pealed off a one hundred dollar bill and handed to Jack. "Here, keep your watch, take this. It should cover your hotel and then some."

"Thanks, man!" Jack exclaimed all glassy eyed. He walked a ways up the boardwalk in a daze. Then turned back toward Russ. "Thanks man!" He said again, still walking and staring at the bill in disbelief. "Thanks!" Pretty soon, he was gone.

Bewildered, Russ watched Jack wander away. *I hope he doesn't go back to the roulette table.* He scratched his head in disbelief. And shrugged as he peered into the pawnshop window. Extraordinary treasures filled the store. One bright shiny silver object caught Russ's generous eye, a Colt Buntline special, under the glass counter. It looked normal in most aspects, a silver single action revolver with black grips but the barrel measured sixteen inches in length.

"Most definitely a long gun," he said to the storekeeper while he thought about Jimmy.

He could see Jimmy's sad eyes when he teased him about his name. "I met this boy on the train up here from Los Angeles. Poor kid's still thinkin' his father's coming home after bein' gone for ten years. I'll buy it and give it to Jimmy as a present, to apologize for my rude comments about his name. It's not the kind of gun that could get the boy in trouble." Russ went on. The storekeeper looked like he couldn't care less.

Chapter Five

"Howdy, Mr. Pots." Jimmy said standing in the Gun Shop door.

"Howdy, Son. Back to find yourself a shootin' iron?"

"Naw. My Aunt said I can't. But I really want to learn to shoot."

"Don't give up Jimmy. You never know what might happen."

Early the next morning Pots went down the street toward Mary Picket's house and the stockyards on an intercept course. As much as he liked Jimmy, any excuse to spend a few moments with Mary seemed like a good idea to him. "Mornin', Miss Mary." He smiled politely.

"Good morning, Potts," She said, suspecting some sort of shuttle diplomacy. "What brings you out this way so early in the mornin'?." She said noticing his bright smile.

"I'm on an errand of mercy."

"I think I know what's on your mind Mr. Rand, but I really don't think shooting lessons is what his ma had in mind."

"Yesterday, Jimmy stopped in at my store. He is very

respectful of you n' his mother. But he also told me about a little incident he had with his friend Aaron. Seems they accidently shot a hole in Aaron's bedroom wall. I guaran-damn-tee you he'll never have another accident like that after I've spent the summer with him at the shooting range. Oops. Sorry about my rough slip of the tongue Miss Mary." He smiled again brightly and respectfully at the lovely young lady.

"Well Mr. Rand I sure don't want to disappoint you. You're so sweet to have such an interest in him. I'll let him know he can go shooting with you."

"Well that will be just fine, Miss Mary." Pots said controlling his excitement. "You have him meet me at my shop at seven tomorrow mornin' n' I'll teach him shoot. I've got a nice Colt he can use 'til he can buy his own."

Jimmy was so excited about his day with Pots he awoke far before his Aunt. He tiptoed through the house attempting to let her sleep. He grabbed two chunks of his Aunt Mary's moist corn bread from the kitchen and then right out the door. The morning was very quiet and crisp with a bit of early morning chill in the air. He arrived at Pots at a quarter to seven in the morning.

"You're early, hey?" Pots asked, "couldn't sleep?

"It seemed like I was practicing in my sleep all night long. Here, I brought you a piece of corn bread that my Aunt made." Jimmy was a thoughtful and generous sort.

Pots grabbed a bag of shooting gear he'd put together

the day before. He led the way, and talked very quietly. The two harmless 'gun-slingers' walked along the dirt streets of early morning Stockton. Pot's shooting range was about three quarters of a mile past the last building heading east out of town. Few people used the range. The ones that did were careful, and kept the area clean. They didn't shoot bottles that scattered broken glass or leave old target cans around that had been punched full of holes.

Pots set out some cans. All loaded and ready to go, he handed Jimmy the Colt Forty Five and said, "there's five rounds in 'er and the hammers sitting on the empty chamber. Let's see what you can do."

Jimmy lifted the gun and held it in one hand. Pots grinned at the awkward child's attempt to look competent. Jimmy cocked the hammer with his thumb. Standing side ways to the targets, with his right arm stretched straight out, his left palm planted on his left hip, he squinted down the barrel and pulled the trigger. The gun bellowed a roaring report and jumped in his hand. Jimmy, astonished by the kick, tried to contain himself. He was unaware of the stunned look on his face. Then Pots spoke up.

"That bullet must've gone clear to Missouri. I didn't see it hit anywhere here in California. Give 'er again; lets see what happens."

Jimmy lifted the pistol again. This time he unconsciously anticipated the kick by jerking forward into the gun, forcing the barrel down. The bullet hit the ground twenty feet in front of the can.

"How 'bout I shows ya how to do 'er right?"

Embarrassed, Jimmy wanted to defend his poor shooting, but he held his tongue and listened as Pots showed him how to hold the gun.

"First, put the butt of the pistol in the palm of your left hand like this," Potts stood close over Jimmy and placed the gun in the boys hand; "and hold the grip with your right hand. Now, tuck your left elbow against your ribs. Hold your right elbow out so's your upper arm is flat."

"No! Come on now! That looks ridiculous!"

"Boy, if you want to learn to shoot, listen and quit your belly achin'. Your left arm, against your ribs, supports the gun up and down. Your right arm supports the gun from side to side."

"I can shoot better fast! I can't shoot fast like that"

"You're not listening to me very well. I thought you wanted me to teach you to shoot. I thought you were gonna learn everything there is to know about guns and shootin'. So listen to me and you'll learn to shoot well, first. Then you can learn to shoot fast, if you still want to."

Jimmy's shooting improved dramatically. Pots had shown him how to look down the sights. They worked on how to squeeze the trigger, rather than pull it, so the shot wouldn't be thrown off. Pots and Jimmy worked until Pots had to open the gun shop.

They walked together to Aunt Mary's house. She was up and cleaning and singing when the guys came up. "Oh my daarling, ohhhhhh my darlinggggggg, oh my darrrrrrrrrrrling Clemin…"

"I hope you'll sing to me like that every morning when were married?" Potts teased.

"Yikes! I didn't hear you come up. Gave me a fright." She said kindly. "I guess I'll have to sing to you every morning when were married." She teased back.

"Oh, brother!" Jimmy complained.

Chapter Six

Old Russ got back on the train in San Francisco, heading to Los Angeles. When the train stopped in Stockton he stepped off. Aunt Mary saw Russ from her office window. He was looking around aimlessly so she walked over to say hello. "Howdy, stranger. I'm Mary Picket. I saw you before on the train north talking to my nephew, Jimmy. Are you lost?"

"Naw. I ain't lost Darlin'. I stopped off, hoping to run across little Jimmy. I had so much fun on the train ride up here. And he was such a nice kid and all excited about shooting. I found this target pistol in a pawnshop in San Francisco. Thought it would be perfect for him, too big to sneak around with and djeeze, it sure is a long gun"

“Well, my goodness, Russ! You are surely kind. But I think this gift is too generous and you shouldn’t.”

“I’m very taken with the boy with’in his good manners and nice disposition, especially towards old gimpy Texas Rangers. I can’t remember the last time I was so appreciated.”

“Jimmy is out at the shooting range with the local gun smith, Mr. Rand. According to Pots, that’s what we call Mr Rand, Jimmy’s become quite a good shot.”

“That’s fine. I’m glad he’s gettin’ good teachin’. Handling a gun takes a lot of practice and a lot more common sense. The train’s leavin’ soon. Could you give this to Jimmy, and tell him Old Russ hit it big in San Francisco? Tell him I thought about him when I saw this.” He handed the long, flat box to Aunt Mary.

Mary took the weighty package. “I’m sure Jimmy will be delighted with your gift.

“Thank you Mary.” Russ shook her hand, and then stepped back up on the train heading south.

The train ride made for a long day. Russ walked up and down the cars for a relief from all the sitting. The flat, beige prairie along the tracks was beautiful but got tedious with no one to talk to. “I could be in Jack’s boots right now if I hadn’t been plain old dumb lucky.” He said to the window.

As Russ’s train pulled in to Coaling Station-A, an immense herd of steers milled along the track. One impressive longhorn steer, solid, bright white, drew Russ's attention. It turned out it was not a steer at all, but a pure white bull. The train, passing very close to the herd as it pulled slowly into the station, gave Russ a clear, close look at the bull's pink lips. The sun, from behind, made its white eyelashes glow and gave the bull an ornery expression.

A generous man at heart, for the first time in his life Russ felt like he could be a big spender. Still standing in the aisle looking at the bull he had a brainstorm of unforeseen magnitude.

The train stopped and Russ jumped right off onto the platform. He strode, with his unusual gate, right up to the cowboy who seemed to be the trail boss.

"Slow down, there buddy! What can I do for you?" The trail boss backed up in case there was something up with this old timer he didn't know about.

"Howdy, sir. I'd like to buy that white bull standing there next to the train tracks."

"I'm sorry sir. That bull ain't f'r sale."

"Everything's for sale, I've heard." Russ told him. "I'll give ya thirty dollars cash money."

The trail boss scratched the back of his head, and pushed his hat up from behind. It fell forward a little, over his brow.

"Oh yea and I'll pay an extra dollar if you put a

Smokin'-T brand on the bull with yer runnin' iron." Russ squatted down and drew a picture in the dust of an oval with a T on the bottom half and three tall skinny S's from the top of the T up to touch the oval.

"How 'bout a horse. I need me a quick 'n easy cow pony and a comfortable saddle."

"Let's see what we can find," the trail boss replied.

They walked way out to the ramuda. Russ picked out the best horse in the herd. "Let me try that skinny little sorrel Filly."

The trail boss threw a bridle on her. Russ took the reins and stood in front of the young horse. He distracted the horse by gently sliding his open hand over the horse's forelock down over her eye. She closed her eye, enjoying the caress.

The trail boss pulled the saddle off his big stock horse and tossed it high on the filly's withers. She bobbed her head a little nervous. Slowly, Russ walked up, grabbed some mane, and stepped up into the saddle. The filly had a very soft mouth and a smooth jog. She'd jump fast into a run, and slide to a ten-cent stop by just wishing back on the reins. Then she'd spin on one hind leg and lope off strong in the opposite direction without an argument.

"I guess she'll do." Russ hid his excitement.

Trail boss said, "She's ten dollars." The trail boss grinned to himself when Russ didn't flinch.

"Ten dollars. Hm. Don't know if she's worth all that."

The trail boss's grin faded, "I don't see that you have a lot of options, old timer."

Russ turned to the trail boss slightly, " Old timer, ya say. Hm. Okay young feller, you just leave that saddle on her, we'll settle up and I'll be on my way."

"Ain't got no extry saddles. It would take two weeks to get a saddle all the way out here."

"Well I can't ride her bare back. I'm too old. And I only got one good knee. If I ever fell off and there weren't no rocks around, I'd be walkin' for sure."

"Go check with the railroad agent," suggested the trail boss.

Whitey had a saddle he'd sell for forty dollars.

"That's robbery," Russ complained.

"Ain't, really. Were m'I goin' to come up with another saddle way out here in the middle of a desert? If the railroad went out of business tomorrow, where'd I be? I'd be stuck. That's where I'd be. I wouldn't be able..."

"Okay. I'll take it. I hope that includes the bit and reins."

Russ settled up with everyone, then saddled up and

drove the bull west, down the wide trail toward San Benito. As he rode, he sang to himself out loud: "I've got a ten dollar horse and a forty dollar saddle come a ti yi yippy yippy yea yippy yea come a ti yi yippy yippy yea. I'm a come ta' Californy, t' raise some long horn cattle, come a ti yi yippy yippy yea yippy yea, come a ti yi yippy yippy yea."

He drove the bull about five miles toward San Benito then stopped and relaxed in his new saddle with one leg hooked over the horn. He didn't know it but he was just a few miles away from Dust Creek. The bull paid little attention to him and munched on the sparse grass. "Alright, Darlin, let's head on back to the depot." Old Russ unhooked his leg, straightened up, gently pulled the sorrel's head around and started back to the depot. Another train back south was going to come along and Russ wanted to be on it. The bright, white bull, with the Smokin' T brand, continued to gnaw grass and ignore the old ranger.

Riding east back to the depot, the sun set behind Russ. The vibrant orange and streaks of blue, gold and white colors in the sky kindled his heart. He stopped again and sat for a long while with his left foot in the stirrup and his right leg hooked over the saddle horn trying to ease the pain in his knee. Gold light bathed his face as he squinted over his shoulder at the horizon, thinking how wonderful his life was.

"Howdy Mr. Whitmore, I'm back. You're the station manager, right? I need a place to keep a horse"

"Yep, I'm in charge. Don't usually board horses."

"I just bought this fine filly for Jimmy Longhon. Sooner or later he should be headin' back here. Can I leave her with you till Jimmy comes home from Stockton?"

"Sure you can. She can stay in one of the cattle pens. I'll throw feed in everyday 'n water's already set up."

"When's the next train to Los Angeles?" Russ wanted to find out.

"The next train south should be through tomorrow afternoon. Take a look here, Russ. What d'ya think of Old Lace?" Whitey took a sip of the whiskey out of the bottle then wrinkled his nose and upper lip and twitched his head.

"I'll pass on that, but thanks." Russ declined Whitey's offer for a sip of the Old Lace. Then Russ proceeded to beat him at checkers until Whitey fell asleep. He leaned backward in the hardwood chair, snoring loudly.

After Whitey passed out from the liquor, Russ wrote a letter to Jimmy.

Dear Jimmy: I sure liked meeting you last month on the train. And since I came into some cash in San Francisco, I decided to invest in our cattle company. I've got a few of my own ideas and hope you don't mind. I bought a white bull right here at the depot from one of the cattlemen. Had him put our Smokin'-T brand on it with a runnin' iron. It ain't perfect but you get the idea. I left the bull on the graze about halfway between Coaling Station-A and San Benito. When you wrangle up some cows, we'll be in business, fifty/fifty pards in the Smokin'-T Cattle Company. I'll register our brand by mail when I get back to the Pueblo. Take care of the filly I left with Mr. Whitmore. I named her Darlin because she's such a sweet little horse to ride. Go ahead and breed her. She's a first class stock horse and the Smokin'-T will need a ramuda. If you've a mind to, make up a branding iron that looks like the brand on the white bull. When I get back through here one of these days, I'll come and find you in San Benito to see how we're doin'. Sincerely, Your Old Pard, Russ Tanner.

Chapter Seven

Back in Stockton, Jimmy opened the box from Russ. His chin dropped almost to his knees. The Buntline was magnificent and strange, and felt front heavy when he held it out in firing position. "Can you believe this, Aunt Mary?" Jimmy hollered. "This is the most crazy gun I've ever seen."

As he held the heavy weapon out, it had a familiar feeling. The memories came back slowly out of nowhere. First he started thinking about the silly look on Lupito's face, refusing to cross the creek and then the big old cap and ball revolver, and his good best friend, Cisco. Sitting on his bed at Aunt Mary's house, he deliberately tried to picture in his mind each action of that horrifying day. The pain wrenched his heart but for some random reasons he wanted to remember.

Jimmy spent the rest of the summer working for old Pots in the gun shop, helping his aunt keep up her yard, and learning to shoot. He never missed a chance to go to the shooting range with Pots or his friends. It didn't take much time before Jimmy was an excellent shot. With his Buntline, off hand he could put five shots in a three-inch circle one hundred yards away. With his Colt single action army, he could put five shots in a three-inch circle at twenty-five yards.

Jimmy took great pride in his shooting. He kept his two guns spotless and well oiled. Pots had taught him how to load his own ammunition. That way, he could control the quality of his cartridges and could make three rounds for the price of one "store-bought" round of ammunition.

Pots was proud of Jimmy. He admired the boy's persistence and attention to detail. Over the summer, a little bit here and a little bit there, Pots gave Jimmy the tools he needed for reloading cartridges as he stumbled across them from time to time in old boxes hidden in the deep, dusty shelves and closets of the gun shop.

The six weeks in Stockton went by in the blink of an eye. Jimmy turned brown from all the work and play out of doors. His hands had developed the tiniest bit of wrinkle, a darker shade of brown and quite a bit of calluses. He had grown at least an inch and had developed a few new muscles. Jimmy had grown into a lanky, weathered young fellow.

One day, while he was out with Pots, Jimmy's Aunt dug out her husband's blue colt and hand-tooled belt. She left it on Jimmy's bed. The back of the holster and belt were made from one piece of leather, nicely worn, but oiled and well taken care of. Too large, the belt wouldn't fit Jimmy's skinny waist. That was a blessing because other wise he might have worn the gun through town and on the train, and, at the age of thirteen, that would have been trouble.

On leaving day, Jimmy packed up all his treasures in a wooden trunk that his aunt gave him. When fully loaded, it weighed over sixty pounds. His aunt borrowed a buckboard. Jimmy and old Pots struggled the trunk up onto the tailgate. Then the three of them squeezed side by side into the wagon seat. They slowly bumped down the road to the Stockton yards and train depot.

Everybody had happy sad eyes, sorry to say goodbye. "Aunt Mary -- Pots," Jimmy stammered, "I don't know how to tell you. I've had so much fun and learned so much here with you both. I hope I can come back again next year and stay all summer." His sojourn to Stockton was the most exciting adventure of his life. He said his goodbyes and heartfelt thanks.

Jimmy and Pots dragged the heavy trunk onto the platform and into the baggage car. When Jimmy stepped up and boarded the train all three of them had wet eyes. Pots and Aunt Mary stood by the tracks watching the steam burst, and the hoot of the whistle, until the train was out of sight.

Even though it was easily within walking distance, Aunt Mary drove the wagon over and dropped Pots off at the gun shop. He was smiling inside and it showed. He grinned at everyone and nobody in particular and didn't think about it. Pots felt delighted with the pleasantries of the comfortable day. First of all, the coming and going of young Jimmy, and then it was not often he spent time with a lovely woman like Mary Picket. Usually his time was spent with cowboys or men who smelled like cowboys. This was the case the following morning. Pots concentrated his attention on replacing a hammer spring in a Colt pistol when two men came into the shop. Without looking up, smiling at his work, Pots said, "How cn'I hep you fella's?"

Usually Pots paid attention to who came in the door. That morning his mind was still with Jimmy and Mary. He looked up to see a terrified man pointing a single shot black powder pistol at his chest. The man shook with fear and his big brown eyes looked as if they would pop right out of his head.

Very skinny, the gunman had a thin beard of jet-black hair and his Adam's apple stuck out unusually far.

"I'll take that Colt right there on the shelf." He said with his voice wavering. It was the silver Colt that Jimmy had practiced with all summer.

A second man, unseen, behind the first chimed in: "And I'll take that Winchester rot thar and you be givin' us two boxes of cotchigis fo bof'm guns."

Pots did what they said. He didn't say a word. The robbers gathered their loot and started out the door. Pots turned to pick up his sawed-off twelve gauge but not quickly enough. Arms full, the skinny one glanced over his shoulder from the doorway. He pointed the single shot pistol under his left elbow and fired. The lead ball caught Pots in the neck, cutting through his jugular vein. The neighbors heard the shot and came running, but old Pots was bleeding profusely. "Is this blood on my hands? It feels like warm milk." He said in a daze of last thoughts. "I'm very sleepy." Finally he sat down on the floor behind the counter, closed his eyes, and never woke up.

Chapter Eight

Dora Longhon, Marcy Cutchel and Elsie Cutchel arrived at the train's Coaling Station-A around noon. Whitey had very few people around and decided to take advantage of the circumstances. He asked the three women to watch the station for a while so he could go visit the neighbors.

When Jimmy got off the train his mother and friends smiled brightly. Jimmy told them all about Pots and Russ. He showed them the "Buntline Special" that was poking out from the good side of a pair of worn out saddlebags.

His mother handed him the letter from Russ. Jimmy struggled through it. The ladies told him it was true; the horse and the bull were for him to take care of.

Jimmy went to see the horse immediately. *How could so much good stuff happen in just one summer?* The filly was striking. The time she had, resting at the depot, had agreed with her. She was filled out and her coat looked sleek and shiny.

Moved by a heart full of gratitude, Jimmy wanted to send telegrams and thank everyone, before he went home.

"We'll go on ahead with your trunk in the wagon. If we don't leave soon it will get dark. You wait here and watch the depot. When Whitey gets back, and you're done sending the telegrams, you can catch up riding in on Darlin." His mother said.

It was dark out when Whitey finally showed up. There was nobody in the telegraph office in Stockton. "Whitey, I'll spend the night here, send my telegrams in the morning. Then I'll get an early start home.

Jimmy was up with the sun, but Whitey wasn't. The morning crept along and it was nine o'clock before Whitey was finally ready to send Jimmy's messages.

Whitey sent the first two telegrams to Pots and Aunt Mary. Then the railroad agent started writing down a message coming back from Stockton.

"Pots dead. Two killers. May be on train. Do not confront."

The message paralyzed Jimmy. He couldn't speak. His light head and pounding heart forced him down into the chair at the telegraph desk. His temper quickly consumed him.

Jimmy's rage came faster and faster, stronger and stronger, crushing his mind like an avalanche of angry, black snow. Blind to reality, all he knew was that he would get even. He loved old Pots and would avenge his death.

Compelled to see who committed the murder, Jimmy stayed at the depot. The train wasn't due into Coaling Station-A until three o'clock. Jimmy tried to stay calm. His delayed trip home worried him all day long. The sound that Jimmy's boots made, around the hardwood floor, annoyed Whitey even more than his fear of confronting the butchers.

Adding to the torment of the hot weather and the waiting, the cicada beetles whined in the trees around the depot. Jimmy paced, fiddled with the checkers and paced some more. Ignorant of what to expect, but resolute, he continued to hang around.

"I'm goin' to sit o'er here at the telegraph desk and act like nothin's unusual if those hombres get off the train. I want you to squat down behind the bar out of sight and stay quiet. Don't be scared. The train will just make a quick stop and then they'll be gone." Whitey instructed Jimmy.

Blinded by anger and hate, Jimmy leered silently into Whitey's eyes and nodded consent.

Finally, the whistle blew. With a distant rumble the train appeared on the horizon. Crouched behind the saloon counter, Jimmy checked the cylinder on his Buntline. Normally the hammer rested on an empty chamber but not today. He wanted the security of the sixth round loaded and ready for anything that might come up.

The moments crept by. Jimmy fidgeted around uncomfortably squatting behind the bar. Finally he peeked out. The bright light of the door was blinding. It seemed to take forever for the train to pull in. When it finally hissed to a stop and lingered, Jimmy thought that nobody would get off. Then the tall skinny assassin with the enlarged Adam's apple walked up to the depot door.

Jimmy peered out over the dark lit bar. From the skinny man's belt, the nickel-plated Colt, that poor old Pots had taught Jimmy to shoot with, reflected the bright morning sun. Right away Jimmy recognized the gun and pointed his Buntline at the murderer's head. The villain turned toward the bar thinking of a drink. His eyes weren't adjusted to the dark room.

Jimmy's voice trembled as he forced out the words, "Where'dyou g-git that Colt, mister?"

Startled by the inquiry, that he assumed came from an older woman, the hooligan stopped in the door. He still couldn't see Jimmy. The lanky man's eyes hadn't adjusted to the dark interior of the depot. He turned his head to see who spoke, his fingers already searching for the pistol's grip sticking out of his pants.

"I bought it in Sacramento."

Jimmy cocked the hammer on the Buntline. The desperado heard the clicks and quickly attempted to make his confession, "Now now! I fou...

The deafening report of Jimmy's Buntline left the skinny man's ears ringing and his teeth clenched, lying on the depot floor bleeding and dying from the concussion. Jimmy wondered if the excruciating pain of the murderer's crushed skull was the last sensation he experienced in life.

The other murderer rushed through the depot door to face the muzzle of Jimmy's long gun pointing at his head.

"Drop the rifle -- Mr. Whitmore here 'ill tie your hands," Jimmy's voice decided to change that day, adding a waiver and tremolo to his demand.

"You're just a kid!" The murderer complained.

Chapter Nine

When the dust settled, Jimmy was a hero for stopping the escape of old Pots' assailants. The ordeal weighed on his mind. But with the support that everyone gave, he slowly warmed back up to his old friends and family in San Benito.

Jimmy was given the two guns taken from Pots' shop in Stockton. Whitey, and everyone concerned thought he had earned them for his bravery. They were not needed for evidence since the second murderer confessed and was hung before he thought to change his story.

Now, with summer over and school started, in his spare time, Jimmy got right to work on the job of building a herd of range cows. With a first rate bull he was eagerly hunting the rest of a herd. With his finances in the state of most thirteen-year old boys, his options were limited. The widow Mrs. Miller had a very old cow. The joke around town was that the poor old bovine walked on three and milked on two. The fact that Mrs. Miller considered negotiating at all made the old cow look pretty good. They struck a deal. Jimmy was to cut, split and stack the widow's firewood for the winter in exchange for the cow. This was a good swap for both of them: Jimmy had no money and the widow would have had to pay somebody to cut her wood.

"You go on and take her Jimmy. I'm tired of milking her anyway," the old lady said quietly and gently.

Jimmy, more satisfied than the widow, went right over to Shorty Small's livery stable. He talked Shorty into helping him make a branding iron. The Smokin'-T brand looked like a T braced inside the lower half of an oval with three smoke curls coming out of the top of the T. They looked like tall, skinny S's. Shorty banged together Jimmy's branding iron from scrap strap metal around the shop. And left it on the workbench where he knew Jimmy would find it.

When Jimmy found the branding iron after school he saddled up Darlin. He rode her over to 'drive' the widow's cow all of the hundred and twenty-five yards down to Shorty's livery stable. He wanted to brand her and set her loose on the range with the white bull.

When Jimmy rode up, the big old cow wouldn't get up. She just lay there chewing on her cud trying to ignore Jimmy and Darlin. The young cowboy, on his neatly groomed steed, thundered up to her several times yipping and whistling. Every time they did,

Darlin almost tripped over the cow. Finally Jimmy got down, tied a war bridle on the cow's oversize head and began to yank on her. Eventually, she labored to her feet, the three that were good. Jimmy left Darlin at the widow's and led his new cow down to Shorty's on foot. Fortunately for Jimmy's pride and reputation, none of the other young cowboys saw him walking the old cow down the street. If they had he would have been forced into some serious explaining to avoid all the teasing he would have been in for.

Jimmy tied the cow to the fence post inside the corral in back of the blacksmith shop. He put the branding iron in the forge and began to ponder just how he was going to accomplish his task. Shorty was not around which left Jimmy to his own imagination. He decided to go right ahead and try it while she stood there tied to the fence post.

When the old cow saw Jimmy coming at her and smelled the glowing, smoking, branding iron, she began to bellow and fuss. She sidestepped away from him when he tried to burn her. Barely touched by the hot iron, she bucked and pulled on the lead rope with all her strength. Persistent, Jimmy tried to hold the hot iron on her hip while she pulled back on the lead rope. Then the fencepost broke off at ground level and whacked Jimmy on the back of his head. The blow knocked him face down into the dust. The old cow limped around the corral, and then she jumped through the broken fence and ran back to the widow Miller's, dragging along what was left of the fence post. Only the top part of the brand had burned enough hide to leave a mark. So the old cow had the smoke half of a Smokin'-T brand burned in her rump, half way to the top of her back. Jimmy watched as she limped home. He grinned with pride and excitement at the thought of a difficult task accomplished.

The little split on the back of Jimmy's head bled gushers down his neck and shirt. He sat in the blacksmith shop doorway with his head in his hands, waiting for the pain to go away. Then Shorty showed up. "What the heck happened here?" With the branding iron laying out in the corral, torn down fence, scuffed up dirt and cow prints trailing out and down to the widow Miller's, Shorty didn't really need to ask any more questions. Calmly, he spat a streamer of dark, tobacco-colored saliva onto the dusty ground.

Shorty wasn't mad, just a little worried about Jimmy's bleeding wound. Standing behind Jimmy he leaned in with interest and checked Jimmy's head. The bleeding had slowed and the cut seemed shallow so nothing else was done to his head. Jimmy's blood soaked shirt looked as though he'd lost enough blood to be dead. But he felt fine, so the two of them went to work fixing the broken fence.

Long Gun

Chapter Ten

-1886-

Walter Freye II arrived in California three summers before. His son, Walt III, was shy around the other kids in town, but he awkwardly tried to make his mark and fit in amongst his peers, routinely to his disadvantage.

The Freyes had purchased the grant of forty thousand acres that started two miles outside of town, and bordered five miles of the south bank of Dust Creek. The elder Freye made it clear to everyone in the territory that he wouldn't restrict the water or access to the Creek.

Every spring, Jimmy's good buddy, Aaron Hochberg, rode out to tend herd with him. Working the cattle meant bobbing the bull calves, sorting culls (of which he had very few) and branding the new calves. Jimmy had made an agreement with Walter Freye II, to trade Jimmy's heifers for heifer calves from the Freye Ranch -- that way the white bull could breed all the Smokin'-T cows and the lineage stayed clean. Little Walt, as Walter Freye the third came to be known, didn't like the agreement Jimmy had with big Walt. Jimmy's herd had done well and by the spring of 1886 he had seventeen head of fine range cattle on the open graze between Dust Creek and the Rail Road tracks.

Wintertime meant rain in the west. The streets in town became deep with mud. Horses and wagons worked the slick clay deeper and deeper. To cross the road in town when on foot, it was best to hunt for shallow spots and jump from clump to clump, avoiding the furrows between the small islands of drier dirt. If a fellow was not careful, the mud would suck a boot right off or go over the top and fill it all the way up.

When the rain let up for a few days, the road began to harden. The shallow spots dried to hard mud and the deep spots dried back into lake-size puddles eight inches deep. Most of the time, the bottom of the puddles stayed pretty firm. It didn't matter. Unless a horse was hungry and going home, he needed plenty of puddle training. The best way was to get a horse through was look right past the puddle and believe it wasn't there. Looking down and wondering if the horse was going to step into it was a sure way to get him to stop, rear, buck or even roll in the mud just for fun. The only way to get through a big puddle was to look on down the road right past it and try to punch holes in the horse with persuasive spurs.

The nice part about the rain was all the wild barley that came up with it. Winter in the west didn't last long. New grass started to grow in December and turned all the rolling hills and valleys vibrant green. By June, the hills turned gold, then fawn then gray-brown.

Jimmy loved the world when the hills turned green. Even though the weather became too cold at times, he preferred it to the scorch of summer.

Elsie Cutchel grew up along side Jimmy. She had no

brothers or sisters and felt self-conscious around people. Partly because of the teasing the boys around town gave her about her buxom figure. Jimmy knew Elsie well and didn't tease her the way the others did. Out of respect for their friendship and the fact that teasing about such things was not a part of his make-up. Her quiet smile and bright, blue eyes kept a subtle but sharp lookout for Jimmy whenever she went out. She disguised strong loving feelings for Jimmy as good friends. She felt protected by the boy she thought of as her counterpart in the scheme of life on the western frontier.

When the land began turning green, like it did every year at that time, fourteen year old Jimmy lost his self-control. He didn't care what the other boys thought. He just couldn't restrain himself from crossing town to visit the Cutchel's.

Elsie's mother had watched Jimmy grow up. She knew Jimmy and his mother very well. And of course, she new about the boy's run ins with trouble. Because he was sincere and far more polite than any other boy in town, and since Elsie never stopped talking about him, she gave him a little more leeway around her daughter. But she still doubted his intentions when he helped unload their buckboard or unhitch their mule. She knew his ulterior motives even though he didn't know them himself, yet. When Marcella Cutchel told Dora Longhon about him helping Elsie wash up dishes after supper, Jimmy's mother couldn't believe it, "Well bless his heart, I don't reckon he's ever washed a dish at our house in all of his fourteen years!"

In the evening while Elsie's mother and father dozed by the fire, Jimmy and Elsie quietly embraced one another for hours. They stood by the washbasin where her parents couldn't see them, and whispered to each other so closely that they shared each other's breath. Jimmy wanted to touch and explore Elsie's body. She wouldn't let him. She wrapped her arms around his neck and gently pressed her forehead against his cheek and held him as close as she could. If Jimmy tried to pull his arms around in front of her, Elsie would squeeze him even tighter so he couldn't. Jimmy melted up as close as possible. He could feel her soft body beneath her dress and smell her hair. He heard her breath, felt her heart beat very hard and they would sway.

Jimmy spent a lot more time with Elsie then. They took frequent walks way out from town in the tall, green barley. Sometimes they would ride double and bareback on Darlin. They would lie back and look up at the deep blue sky and kiss and talk and laugh. Jimmy tried to undo Elsie's dress buttons and she played him away.

"If you really love me, you'll wait 'till we're married." She said and looked deeply and seriously into his eyes.

One sunny afternoon, after seeing each other everyday for months, unfamiliar feelings came over Elsie. She began to notice the shape of his hips, the width of his shoulders, and the lean muscular tendons of his arms. She couldn't stop thinking about him. The next time they sat in the tall grass and he fiddled with the top button on her dress she said, "I love you, Jimmy." Her heart pounded, sighs of arousal escaped as she attempted to control her breath. "Go ahead, I won't stop you."

Jimmy tilted his head and lifted his eyebrows and gave her a surprised questioning look. "You mean like this?" he teased, and plucked at her buttons again.

Jimmy never intended to make Elsie sad. She didn't look sad. She wasn't smiling, but she wasn't frowning. She just looked up at his eyes. Her cheeks were rosy. Her lips flushed red and waited for another kiss. Her eyes sparkled with passion. Jimmy was still having trouble with her top button.

When he finally fumbled the top buttons open on her dress he found something he was not expecting. Around Elsie's neck dangled a silver chain. On the chain above her breast hung a silver locket the shape of two hands in prayer.

When Jimmy found the sentinel locket, his first impulse was to quickly button Elsie back up. But something inside wouldn't let him stop. His curiosity took over and he opened the rest of her buttons to her waist. Then he carefully lifted back the lapels of Elsie's dress. He was in awe and couldn't pull his eyes away. He thought his heart would beat right out of his chest. He could hardly breathe and he felt momentarily sick to his stomach.

"You're so beautiful," he gasped.

Elsie could hardly hold back from laughing at Jimmy's expressions of worry and desire. He looked at her and her eyes smiled yes, and filled with tears.

Without any other experience in the matter, Jimmy didn't know what to do. After his brief examination he said, "I'll always love you, Elsie," and quickly buttoned up her dress, still happy to have seen her lovely young body. For the rest of the warm, sunny afternoon, they sat deep in the tall, green, wild barley that towered against the sky, talking and laughing and holding each other's hands.

Jimmy didn't tell his mother about his feelings and playful love with Elsie so he wrote another letter to old Russ in Los Angeles. He told Russ he loved Elsie and wished to marry her and how strong his desires burned for her.

Russ wrote back promptly as usual and told Jimmy if Elsie was to be his wife it wouldn't matter how long they waited. If they went ahead and she wasn't meant to be his, the Good Lord had ways to punish, in a way his young mind couldn't imagine. He told him to wait and enjoy the fires and desires; they are a grand part of life to treasure, and experience. To extinguish them too soon would calm a thrilling time of his life that he might never get back.

Jimmy loved Russ's letters. They cleared his mind about Elsie. He loved her but he didn't have to rush out and marry her. Russ was respectful, with a strange combination of philosophy and humor and a view of life that no one in San Benito had to offer.

Long Gun

Chapter Eleven

People out on the western frontier depended heavily on wild game for food. As a teenage boy, Jimmy was expected to go out hunting to help support his mother. Jimmy loved this time alone and didn't look upon it as a chore at all.

In the winter, ducks and geese flew through their territory. Jimmy liked to hike along Dust Creek, surprising the waterfowl that stopped there.

Both banks of Dust Creek were accepted as common land. Stockmen used the water for their cattle. Mothers took their children there on picnics. Teenage boys hunted and prospected for gold along it. Even though no countable gold was ever found, most of the boys tried panning at least once in their lives.

Jimmy hunted with a muzzle-loaded, ten-gauge shotgun. It was slow to load and painful to shoot. With only one shot, Jimmy was very careful. He hid quietly in the brush along the bank. He let the birds come in quite close before he fired.

Little Walt, who was six feet tall, happened to be hunting on the same morning as Jimmy. They could see each other a half-mile away along a raised portion of the bank. They continued toward each other. Jimmy thought they would walk past without a thought. When they were twenty feet apart however, Little Walt lowered his fancy German Drilling. He pointed the fancy, three barreled long gun at Jimmy's chin.

"I know you think you're the big shot shootist around here. Well, I don't care. I've got you dead in my sights. Don't make any stupid moves or else. This is my family's land, and I don't want you hunting around here ever again."

Shocked and furious by Walt's rude behavior, Jimmy stood frozen, thoughtful and fearful. *"Everyone hunts this land, if he looks away I'll pull up and let 'im have one in the face, then I'll be in trouble 'cause nobody'll know he started this thing"*, these and more silent thoughts echoed around in Jimmy's head.

Frightening, foul arrogance lingered on the older boys face. The younger Jimmy knew better than to argue into the wrong end of a shotgun. He was sure Walt wouldn't shoot but didn't risk a test of his theory.

Without saying a word, Jimmy hung his head low, turned on the narrow trail and marched along the creek back to town rehearsing in his mind all the things he would say to Little Walt if he got the chance and found the courage. After about five minutes that seemed like an hour, he looked back over his shoulder. Walt stood crooked in the golden evening sun. He leaned on the heavy gatepost at one end of the barbed wire fence that delineated the Freye's land. With his weight on one leg, his fancy long gun cradled in his arms, Walt looked as menacing as he perceived himself to be.

With the kind of money that Walt's family had, Walt dressed a little nicer and had his hair cut more frequently than most of the boys in San Benito. He rode around on bigger, faster horses with shinier, newer saddles and fancier trappings. His parents had high expectations of him, and required strict manners from him that he doled out with the good of himself foremost on his mind. So, to the young ladies around San Benito, at least on the outside, he appeared to be a very appealing package.

Elsie, like most girls around town, noticed Walt right off. He was the topic of many female conversations.

Walt had taken a shine to Elsie. At first, she ignored him, remembering too well the anger she felt the day he teased her on the boardwalk with her dime. But he persistently smiled and tipped his hat to her every chance he found. His manners and clothes and fine horses finally turned her head.

When the spring picnic and hoedown appeared on the social horizon, Walt invited Elsie. Jimmy however assumed Elsie would come with him. When he caught wind that she intended to go with Walt, he didn't bother to check with her and became thoroughly disheartened. He had always thought of Elsie as his girl. And this news was a crippling disappointment for Jimmy.

"Djeeze," he said quietly one day when he saw her on the street. "I thought you were my girl."

"You don't own me, Jimmy." She said, "I didn't think you were going. Especially since it's out at the Freye's place. I know how you feel about Little Walt."

Jealousy and confusion put Jimmy completely out of sorts. He couldn't concentrate on anything except to figure out what Elsie could be thinking about, with such a low life excuse for a man as Little Walt.

When the afternoon of the dance came around Jimmy went about his day knowing he wouldn't go. "Oh my goodness. Jimmy, you listen hea'. Elsie ain't married to Little Walt. You'll have a chance to talk and dance with hur. Fact is, you'll probably steal hur right away from him." So, with a little trickery, Callidora Longhon persuaded her son to attend.

At twilight Jimmy rode out to the Freye's ranch alone, nervous and thinking about what he would do once he arrived.

"Now here's a man to be reckoned with," Shorty started up. "Everybody be careful now he might be packin' a long gun." He squatted and spread his arms pretending to steady himself. Lolo the barber, sat listening but quiet on the water trough next to the horse hitching line made of a heavy extended rope.

"The Scourge of the West f'r sure," Whitey added.

"Ah, come on now, you ain't gon' t' start that again now are ya? Whitey tell him I ain't got no gun with me," Jimmy shyly protested.

A couple of hundred people were all talking, eating, dancing, and drinking at the same time. Jimmy felt out of place. Even the lively melody of the fiddle, that he loved to hear, didn't improve his mood. After having a little to eat, he decided to leave before he caught sight of Elsie with Walt.

The sun had gone down the rest of the way. Jimmy led Darlin around the Freye's big barn to head home, from inside the barn, he heard Elsie upset and shouting, "Stop it, Walt! You just stop that right now!"

Jimmy took a gander inside to see Elsie struggling to get away from Walt.

When she saw Jimmy and Darlin walking past the big barn doors, she lurched away from Walt, "Jimmy!" she lifted her voice, "please -- get me out of here. Take me home." Knowing Jimmy was irritated at her, she wasn't sure he'd help.

But the opportunity to show off one's shiny armour didn't come around too often.

Walt had grabbed Elsie roughly by the upper arm and pulled her back, shoving her down into the hay on the dirty floor behind him. The rough treatment Walt dealt to Elsie was more than Jimmy could tolerate. He rushed up to Walt's fists with teeth clenched.

"You can't treat her like that!"

Both boys turned hot with anger. Their hearts pounded and their voices trembled as they cursed at one another. Walt kicked at Jimmy but missed, churning up dust.

"This is my barn, my property; get out, Long Gun!"

From previous experience he knew calling Jimmy by that name, "Long Gun" made him very mad.

"Don't call me that! You low life son of bitch." He tried to go around Walt to help Elsie up. Walt chested his way between them, whirled and swung in a fury, hitting Jimmy high on the side of the head.

"Stop it, Walt! Stop it right now!" Elsie screamed.

By then, some of the other guests heard her and came into the barn to see what was going on. Jimmy and Walt were both filthy from rolling in the dry hay and dust on the barn floor.

Elsie, a little disheveled, her new dressed garnished with dirt and straw, tucked her chin, pouted her lower lip out farther than physically possible, and took Jimmy's arm. She struggled to hold back her tears of embarrassment. She knew she had upset Jimmy. She realized what a lout Walt could be. But even after all the commotion, she still had oddly tender feeling for Walt as well as Jimmy.

"Please take me home." She forced a whisper to Jimmy through painfully persistent but quiet tears.

She didn't look anyone in the face as Jimmy walked her through the audience. They went over to Darlin who wrinkled her brow and watched Elsie walk up. Darlin showed a little humorous concern with Elsie's tears, the way horses unwittingly do. Then, without warning, Darlin gave Elsie a big slobber hello right on her face. Elsie recoiled and wiped her face with her sleeve. Darlin bobbed her head as if she wanted to laugh. Jimmy stiffened and shoved the horse's big head away, then bridled her, tightened the cinch and gave Elsie a leg up.

Jimmy walked and led Darlin while Elsie rode for a little way. Then, standing with his chest at Elsie's thigh, he took her foot out of the stirrup. "What are you doing?" she chirped and pulled her foot from his hand. Smiling to himself at her dramatic overreaction, he put his foot in the stirrup, stepped up easily and swung around behind Elsie. She felt good in his arms. His warm breath on her neck tingled. She leaned back into his arms at the sensation. "Mmmmm," she responded to his breath. They didn't say anything to each other the entire four miles back to town.

At the Cutchel's place, Jimmy lifted his leg over and slipped down the side of Darlin's rump. He politely helped Elsie off the horse. She quickly leaned toward her house to go in. But abruptly she stopped and turned. Wrapped her arms around Jimmy's neck and nearly squeezed the breath out of him.

"Hold me." She whispered, "Never stop holding me, Jimmy."

Chapter Twelve

Little Walt was jealous and humiliated about what happened at the party. It was three days later when he went into town seeking Jimmy. Walt brought his father's gold plated colt with polished pearl grips. "I'm not going to load it in case it goes off by accident." He told one of the hired ranch hands. "I just want to scare him. Then Elsie'll see who's the better man."

Jimmy hadn't made a habit of wearing a gun. He remembered what Russ told him on the train, *"It was just too heavy and awkward and got in the way for work."* It was a good thing he didn't have one on the day Little Walt marched into the blacksmith shop. Jimmy concentrated on straightening out a pair of old horseshoes. He was about to re-bend them the other way to make himself a pair of spurs. Hearing footsteps Jimmy looked up. Little Walt strode in with the gold Colt's hammer cocked. Jimmy thought Walt meant to kill him this time and was scared senseless.

"Elsie is going to be my gal, Long Gun. It'd be best if you just stay away from her. Next time this gun 'ill be loaded." He snapped the hammer on an empty chamber and Jimmy flinched wildly to get out of the way, expecting to be shot at point blank range.

Jimmy reached out quickly and grabbed the pistol out of Walt's hand.

"Your pa'll have a lot of use for this dandy Colt when I get finished with it." Jimmy said.

He began beating it against the anvil violently. Then with Shorty's rounding hammer he flattened the barrel and severely dented the cylinder until it wouldn't turn.

He threw it back at Walt. "If you ever come within shooting distance of me again, you'd better be ready for a real fight, Freye!"

Jimmy's mind experienced an overload. *"What kind of world do I live in?"* he agonized over what to do about Little Walt.

There had been violence as long as he could remember. He decided he had no choice now but to start wearing his guns.

Chapter Thirteen

Over the years since Russ and his Aunt gave him the guns, they stayed in the trunk from Stockton, except for target practice. He still had the silver Colt .45 he inherited after Pots' death.

Working with Shorty's tools and leather scraps, that he begged and borrowed from all his friends, Jimmy fixed up his uncle's old gun-belt into a first class yet unusual holster set up.

The belt hung high on his left hip and low on his right. He had sewn another holster on the left side of the belt with softened rawhide. The old holster that was already attached to the belt on the right hung low, outside of his right thigh. The new holster on the left faced backward for the Buntline. The Buntline hung backward leaving the handle out front. He could reach across in front of his belly with his right hand. Grabbing the handle, pulling the long barrel out and sliding it across, there was little more movement needed to point the gun into firing position.

Unconsciously, taking some of old Pots' philosophy and adding it to his own, he rehearsed his clarification defending his awkward holster rig, *"I'd rather take my chances with a little more time to aim, a lot farther away, than be too close to any sidewindin' gun slinger who's more n' likely got all his courage from a bottle. Prob'ly dependin' mostly on up close luck 'n surprise, rather 'n skill, or he wouldn't be drawin' down on some poor poke like me to begin with."*

The low holster on his right hip tied down to his thigh was for quick draw up close shooting. There he kept old Pots' silver Colt. Not a coward by any means, he gave considerable thought on how he would handle himself if forced into a showdown with Little Walt.

He knew a lot about shooting, sight picture, accuracy of loads and consistency in stance and holds. Little Walt did not. Spending three or four hours a week at target practice, Jimmy was a crack shot. Anyone in San Benito would say that he was the best shot around. Not full of himself, he decided to leave rather than risk killing Little Walt.

Never in his entire life had he ever twirled a gun on his finger. He took his shooting seriously. He kept his guns clean, never showed off, and up to this point in his young life, had never worn them in public. Nor was he wearing them the day he Left Shorty's shop and walked across town to find Elsie with her arms over her head hanging out laundry.

"Elsie -- ?"

"Hey Jimmy." She smiled and ducked her head sideways shyly, the way that sent his heart pounding many times before.

Today his heart pounded but for a different reason. "Elsie, I'm headin' south for a trip to the The Big Pueblo de Los Angeles tomorrow. I'm goin' ta find ol' Russ. Tell him about the Smokin'-T cattle and the trouble I'm havin' with Little Walt. 'N see what he has ta' say."

Elsie's lower lip started to curl and quiver uncontrollably before Jimmy even said the word Russ. Tears welled up in her eyes. Lowering her head leaning forward she threw her arms around his neck sobbing. Over the years she had seen most of the young men about Jimmy's age leave San Benito and never come back.

Jimmy felt the wetness of her eyes soaking into his shirt and neck. "I'll be back sooner than you know Els'. Don't cry. If I get into it with Little Walt, maybe he gits killed; then I might be hung and *really* never see you again."

She couldn't help herself. She was shocked at his news. She sulked, and stared into the dark of his shirt with her faced tucked into his chest. Her throat so tight she was barely able to choke out her loud whisper. "Oh Jimmy, don't go." She could hear her own voice like a soft echo, muffled by his shirt and neck.

He saddled up Darlin early the next day. His mother stuffed as much jerked venison, biscuits, and apples as would fit without falling out, into his saddlebags. He wanted to travel light, so he steered clear of bringing along a packhorse. He rode east to Coaling Station-A, in the dark gray early morning light.

Darlin was eager to go. She loved working the Smokin'-T cattle, and acted like that was where they were headed. Passing the herd and staying on the trail bothered the mare. She balked, perked her ears, and turned her head to stare intently at the cattle. She bobbed her head briskly, wanting to lope to the cattle.

"I know you think those doggies need chasin', girl, but that ain't what we're up to today," Darlin slowed her walk considerably as they passed the herd. She toddled the rest of the day, wanting either to chase the cattle or return home.

The depot at Coaling Station-A had a new building added, aligned with the old office and bar. The new warehouse and store sheltered spools of wire, kegs of nails, and about anything a rancher needed to make life easier. Coming up with cash to pay for it was tough for most of the citizens of San Benito. Accustomed to the primitive life, they used rawhide leather for almost everything from hinges to ropes.

Jimmy parked Darlin on the green grass growing around the water trough. He untied a pair of rawhide hobbles from the saddle, hopped down, and buttoned the hobbles on Darlin's front feet so she wouldn't run home or back to the cattle. He took off her bridle so she wouldn't tangle in it, and then walked into the old depot. Darlin watched Jimmy as he paced away, and then bent down to enjoy the fresh green grass.

"Hey Mr. Whitmore, how's life out here nowadays?"

"Blow me down, young Mr. Longhon, Scourge of the West. Ain't had much excitement around here since you rode the train from your Aunt's and fetched us those interlopers from Stockton. What brings you out here today?"

"I'm headin' for the big pueblo t' see old Russ Tanner."

"Heard he's doin' well for himself down there. He invested his winnings from San Francisco in a hotel right on the main street and is making a killin' runnin' a roulette wheel, cards, bar, and a fine dining establishment."

"Yes sir." Jimmy Said. "'n we're pards in the Smokin'-T cattle company too."

"How many head ya runnin' now'days?" Whitey asked.

"Well, not enough to brag about Mr. Whitmore. So's I guess I'll be needin' tickets for Darlin and me, through to Los Angeles." Jimmy said, changing the subject.

"How's that filly treatin' you, boy?"

"She ain't a filly no more; she's given me two fine foals and is carryin' another now."

"It'll be three dollars for the both of you, Jim boy."

After paying for his ticket, Jimmy borrowed a brush and clippers from the depot's tack shed, unsaddled Darlin and spent an hour cleaning her up. The train pulled in at five in the evening. Jimmy led Darlin up the wooden cattle ramp, into the empty open-slat livestock car. Jimmy tied her to the side to keep her from running around inside the car and falling if the train lurched.

Over his shoulder, he lifted the saddle, still wet and smelly from Darlin's sweat and the long ride to the depot. Picking up the saddlebags, he clomped up the boardwalk onto the train. Nobody else was on board. He flopped the saddle on the floor across the aisle. He stretched out on his back, pulled the Buntline from his belt and laid it on his chest. He closed his eyes, and was soundly sleeping before the train was two miles south of the depot.

Startled by the train's whistle, Jimmy opened his eyes. The sky outside the window was inky black. A haze in the air dimmed the stars. A lantern lit white letters on the wall of a building "Pueblo de Los Angeles."

Darlin' paced in place, alert and nervous, as Jimmy walked up. She had spent many years on the trail and felt secure in the wilderness. This was different. She'd never been this far from home before, with so many strange buildings and scents. She whinnied for Jimmy, calling him to soothe her brittle nerves.

The Pueblo had a distinct aroma: the combination of

food cooked in the open air, burning garbage, livestock manure and the faint scent of urine.

Jimmy saddled up Darlin'. He swung up, but Darlin' trotted off before he got settled. He guided her up to an open passenger-car door where the conductor stood.

"Can you tell me how to find the Hotel de Los Angeles?"

"See this road you're standing on? Follow it south until you find the next main road and go right. If you come up on the reeds of the cienegas, you've missed the road and gone too far. Anyway, follow that road into town and you won't be able to miss the Los Angeles. It's the largest building around."

"Thank you sir."

They trotted off. Darlin' looked from side to side and called out with a long whinny. The local horses, mules and dogs answered, which made her more nervous.

Turning at what appeared to be a road, Jimmy and Darlin' came to a dead end at a small adobe house. An angry dog barked and came after them. Darlin' spun around and loped away with the mangy animal close on her heals. A man's voice yelled out, "Carumba niños! Chucho! Ven aqui!" crisp against the silent background of the sleeping village.

Back at the road, Jimmy turned Darlin' to the right and right again at the next set of ruts. The village seemed very quiet with no one around. He heard the muffled hiss and rumble of the idling train in the distance. The first hint of morning made a silhouette of the Hotel against the extremely dark gray-orange sky. An old man stepped out from the adobe across from the hotel and stared at Jimmy suspiciously.

Standing in a muddy puddle where a lot of horses had stood, Jimmy tied Darlin' to the hitching rail in front of Russ's hotel. He sat down on the bench on the high boardwalk, waiting for the day to begin.

He thought of how dirty the village appeared compared to San Benito. There were many vacant lots between the adobe buildings. Broken wagon wheels, pieces of canvas, and other junk littered the lots. Next to some of the homes, there were piles of rusty cans, bottles and jars. The large population apparently used up much more of the resources and left waste difficult to handle.

Jimmy sat in front of the hotel as the morning light slowly intensified. The village of Los Angeles was coming to life. Two old ladies with dark shawls over their head and shoulders, walked side by side up the street, balancing terra-cotta jugs on their heads.

A lovely young woman came out onto the boardwalk from within the hotel, her skirt, blouse, and hair disheveled. A tall slender young man of brown complexion and high cheekbones sauntered out of the hotel behind her.

The young man wore a very large, black sombrero,

tilted high on the back of his head. Black, tight fitting wool pants detailed the shape of his figure. The pants met a tiny jacket made of matching material high on his waist. The girl left prints in the dust when she walked across the street barefoot. She disappeared into an adobe house across from the hotel. The young man followed her into the street. A rooster crowed in the distance. Darlin' whinnied and bobbed her head. The attractive young lady reappeared in the doorway of the adobe holding a double-barreled shotgun, "Salga aquí." She said sternly but quietly.

The young man turned around candidly and sauntered away.

Jimmy sat and watched. There were so many more people here than in San Benito. Then he stood up, walked to the hotel's window. Cupped his hands around his face against one of the small glass panes and looked into the hotel. The lobby was empty. Chairs and barstools were stacked on top of the tables in the deserted saloon.

Feeling restless, Jimmy tightened Darlin's cinch strap and stepped up into the saddle. They took a walk and looked around the village. Two dirty-faced little boys stood in the doorway of their adobe house. The crisp orange glow of the morning sun sparkled in their brown eyes as they watched Jimmy pass.

From the top of the rise, Jimmy noticed a line of cottonwood trees snaking along below him. They formed the boundary of the Rio de Los Angeles. At the entrance of a trail through the brush, a sign read

"No Baño." Jimmy thought this was peculiar as he rode across the coarse sand into the shallow clear water. Darlin' stretched her neck down and took several long draughts.

Standing for a while in the shallow water, Jimmy and Darlin' watched the beautiful young lady walk up, stealing glances at them with black, curious eyes. He remembered her leaving the hotel earlier that morning. Her wavy, long, loose black hair dangled over her shoulders, slightly touching the surface of the river, as she filled a terra-cotta jug with water. She lifted it and balanced it on her head, and walked away along the trail. As she walked away, he wondered if anyone in the village wore shoes.

Jimmy felt restless. Uninvited, thoughts of Elsie were coming to mind. He wished he could see her and hold her and listen to her whisper his name.

Three small, energetic pigs, concentrating on the trail with their squinty eyes, squeaked and clamored their way to the water. After plopping down here and there searching for the perfect spot, they rolled in the shallow mud. Thrusting their noses into the wet bank, they covered themselves as best they could with sandy mud. Seeming satisfied they relaxed in their comfortable hideout.

Jimmy pressed his legs against Darlin's sides. He reined her around back across the water and up the same trail the young lady had taken away from the river.

More people were stirring around their small homes.

The aroma of beans and carnitas stimulated his appetite. Returning to the hotel, he tied Darlin' to the hitching rail once again.

He opened the saddlebags and rummaged for food. Finding three spicy chunks of dried venison, an apple, and a biscuit, he made himself comfortable on the hotel bench.

He heard somebody inside the hotel begin to arrange chairs and stools on the wooden floor. He could see another man through the window, yawning behind the hotel counter, putting mail into the pigeonhole slots lining the wall. He hoped it was Russ, but it wasn't.

Jimmy fed the core of his apple to Darlin'. Then he wiped the oil off of the dried venison and Darlin's slobber onto his pants.

Timidly, he entered the hotel and walked to the desk.

"Howdy, sir, d'you know were I'd find Mr. Tanner?"

Apprehensively, the clerk eyed Jimmy's unusual gun belt and unkempt appearance.

"What's your business, son?" He asked curtly.

"I'm Jimmy Longhon, an old friend of his." He fingered the butt of his pistol as he said, "He gave me this Buntline five years ago in Stockton."

The clerk winced when Jimmy touched the gun and disappeared around the corner. Jimmy wandered around the hotel lobby and restaurant, curiously inspecting the elegant detail in the furniture and woodwork. After many minutes he sat down on a stuffed chair close to the window and stared sleepily out at the street.

After what seemed a lifetime, he heard boots upstairs coming his way, getting louder with each rapid step. Then Russ appeared at the glossy, white rail on the balcony above.

"Jimmy! I don't believe my eyes, you're all growed up." The rounded innocence of twelve had given way to an honest, lean young cowboy.

Russ moved down the steps as rapidly as his old legs could carry him. Impossible as it might be, Russ seemed older as well. He looked as old as dirt when Jimmy first met him five years before, and now he looked older than that.

"I don't feel any more grown than the last time I saw you in Stockton." Jimmy said, glad to see old Russ and unable to stop smiling. "I've got Darlin' with me."

Russ grabbed Jimmy by the right hand, pulled him close and wrapped his left arm around his shoulder and hugged him tight. Jimmy's youthful strength felt good to Russ. He had only spent one day with the boy five years before, but now they were as close as family.

"Has that ornery white bull killed anybody yet?"
"Well, nah, he ain't so bad. Now the Smokin'-T's got seventeen head on the range, four steers, twelve cows,

and that ol' bull 'El Toro, Blanco-Grande', that's what me'n Aaron calls him for short." Jimmy grinned and wagged his head, proud of his joke. "I've been tradin' calves with the Freye Ranch so's to keep the lines clean."

"Sounds like the Smokin'-T's doin' right fine, Jimmy. I'm real glad you felt like coming down here in person to catch me up on the business. How d'you like the hotel? I watched them hotels in San Francisco rakin' in all that money with their Roulette tables and thought I'd try it myself. Let me tell you, people work harder at tryin' to git somethin' for nothin' and losin', than they do at their own trade. If they'd work half as hard at a payin' job, they'd be millionaires. Let's eat some breakfast. All this excitement's made me hungry."

Without explaining that he already ate, Jimmy followed Russ out the hotel doors and to the right. The hotel occupied a corner building. They walked along the boardwalk around the corner in a direction Jimmy hadn't explored yet. High on the wall of the building connected to the hotel was a large green, yellow and red sign that said Cisco's Cafe. Again, the caring in Russ's old heart had found its' way into the world. "I knew, sooner or later, you'd show up here in Los Angeles. I'd surprise you with the café named after your old amigo." Russ explained with pride and excitement.

Russ and Jimmy sat down at a table next to the windows. A Mexican girl came to the table to take their order.

"Rosa, this here's my good friend Jimmy Longhon from San Benito. Put any food the boy eats on my bill, and gueremos heuvos, fruita and leche de schiva por favor." His accent was very gringo. He didn't care nor did anybody else.

"Si, Señor Russ" The young lady nodded tenderly, then peeked quickly into Jimmy's eyes. Shoulders back with her best posture, she smiled, turned, and walked back to the kitchen.

She was the most beautiful young lady Jimmy had ever seen. Her hair clung to the back of her head in a bun. A few loose curls hung seductively by her temples. She wore a long, fluted, white skirt with tiny flowers embroidered in white around the bottom. Her ruffled, white blouse sat off her shoulders and revealed the silky, brown skin of her neck, chest, and back.

Jimmy remembered Rosa and felt uncomfortable, "I saw that girl at the river this morning and comin' out of the hotel before that. She stuck a shotgun out of the house across the street at some fella' followin' her."

"Don't mind her. She's the local beauty. Her ma, Carmelita Ramirez, cooks for me here. My two buildings connect at the kitchen. It serves the hotel restaurant for supper and the café for breakfast and lunch. The boy is Victorio Machado. He wants Rosa to marry him. But she can't make up her mind. I think she might have to shoot him if she decides not to be his wife. What are your plans for the rest of the day?"

He thought about it for a minute, "I don't have any

plans. I came down here to talk to you about a problem I'm havin' in San Benito."

"Well, tell me. It must be a perty big problem to bring you all this way."

" Well I wanted to see you, besides that," he said, defending his situation. "But there's this fella, kind of a dude, his father trades calves with me. We call him Little Walt. His father is Walter Freye II."

"I've heard of the Freyes and you told me about 'em in your letters. The old man's supposed to be a square dealer, lots o'money."

"That's them. Little Walt's threatened me twice now, guns in my face. I knew he weren't plannin' to shoot, but I'm 'fraid someday soon he'll quit kiddin' around. If I was to shoot Little Walt, my tradin' days with the Freyes would be over. And could be, they'd hang me too."

"I see your point. Runnin' away from a fight can be easier than facin' it at..."

"I weren't runnin', Russ. I ain't afraid of Little Walt. It's more likely I'm afraid he'll force me to kill . . . ah heck!"

Jimmy's throat tightened up. "I gotta go out back for a minute." He croaked.

Looking away from Russ, he scuffed his chair back and walked to the door. Jimmy thought that Russ didn't understand that he wasn't afraid of Walt, just afraid of what he might do to Walt. Feeling helpless with nobody else to turn to he couldn't hold back any longer. Slumping down on the edge of the boardwalk, he covered his face with his hands and bawled.

Quietly, Rosa stepped up behind him and said. "Senior, su comida es a la mesa." She knew he was crying but didn't mention it, partly out of fear and respect, and partly out of empathy. It took a lot to make the men of Los Angeles tear up, and violent explosions of anger could result from bringing it to their attention.

It wasn't uncommon, living in California in the eighteen hundreds, to pick up and speak a little Spanish, "Si, muchas gracias." He replied not turning his head.

Before reentering the café, Jimmy made one more careful wipe at his eyes, in an attempt to hide any evidence of his emotions. The table now contained food fit for a fiesta. At Jimmy's place and in front of Russ, rested two huge clay plates overflowing with beans, tortillas, and potatoes, covered with spicy red salsa. Poached in a kettle of the same red salsa, two huge eggs were floating dead center on each of the plates. Behind each plate sat a clay mug of cool goat's milk. In the middle of the table between the two amigos sat another plate of sliced melons, oranges, and berries. And if that were not enough, there was still another clay platter covered with linen. Under the steaming linen, six more hot hand-made tortillas were hiding. Jimmy felt full just looking at the table.

"Now, how does that make you feel?"

"Whoa, Russ! I've never seen so much food on one table, in my whole life!"

It was true. He hadn't. The pace of life in Los Angeles required less work and more time. Time to enjoy the food, the sun, the ocean, and the beautiful women. Like the proud, puffed up roosters running around in the morning sun, the men of Los Angeles took great pride in their clothing and appearance, far more than the men of San Benito. The women took great pride in their cooking, their beauty and their generous love for life.

Jimmy and Russ applied themselves to their meal and handily devoured everything that Rosa had brought.

"Esta bien?" She asked, leaning to pick up the empty tortilla plate. As she leaned, Jimmy turned bright red. With all his strength he tried not to look, but he couldn't control his eyes. Her young brown breasts, softly lit by the window light filtering through her blouse, teased his eyes. His heart pounded so vigorously he was sure she could hear. She, of course, couldn't hear his heart, but she knew what she had done. She was well in control of where and when her body and blouse teased her men.

"I assume you'd rather stay here and keep Rosa company, but how 'bout mañana you join me on a trip 'bout sixty miles south of here, to the Rancho Santa Margarita y Las Flores? I've got to see ol' Doc O'Neill about some beef."

Jimmy blushed again. "Sure, that sounds fine to me." He was now uncomfortably full of food and in pain, but wouldn't show a hint of it to Russ.

From inside the kitchen, Rosa watched as they left. When she had leaned to pick up the tortilla plate, her heart actually pounded harder and longer than Jimmy's. Carmelita could tell by her actions how Rosa felt about the new gringo. She smiled to herself, remembering her own young brown body. How the men stole surreptitious glimpses and hid wanton thoughts behind expressions of innocence.

Rosa walked quickly to catch Jimmy before he disappeared. "Will you come and see me tonight for a walk along the river? My mother is going to see her boyfriend. When the lights are out in the kitchen, come across the street to my house." She knew he knew her little adobe across the street.

Distracted but happy to be in Los Angeles, Jimmy spent the day following Russ through his circadian routine. That evening from the saloon he slipped away. "Rosa!" He whispered. A second passed as he listened intently. "Si." She whispered back. The wool blanket covering the door space moved to the side revealing Rosa's long black hair framing her blushing face. "Ola, Jaime." She whispered and took him by the hand. The warm glow of forty candles set on the clay floor completely filled the room. Rosa's adobe was a mystical world, fraught with the hint of passion.

"Come close me." She said unable to fully translate

her feelings and pulled him down to her on the bed. With one moment of awkwardness and no other way to communicate, Rosa smiled and blinked teasingly, directly into Jimmy's eyes. Slowly, they leaned together. Gently they caressed each other, exploring one another's sensitive skin. Trembling with passion, they kissed softly, then harder and harder. Looking into Jimmy's eyes, Rosa untied the bow holding the top of her blouse around her neck. Returning her gaze, he reached up and pulled her collar wide, exposing her beauty.

"Kiz me, Jaime." She demanded.

He kissed her soft brown neck and continued his lips down her shoulders. She leaned back closing her eyes and lifted her arms over her head enjoying his exploitation. He pulled at her sensitive skin with his teeth. She took the back of his head and manipulated his hands and mouth for her own pleasure. When she moaned, he repeated his actions vigorously. Quivering in his grasp, she satisfied herself.

When her murmurs subsided, he moved over her. Watching her writhe, beguiled by her exotic Latin beauty, ensnared by her passion, she inflamed his fiery flesh. Encouraging his advances the way she did, tormented him.

Outside the wool blanket, Victor's voice whispered politely, "Rosa, es que usted?."

"You mus' go." She whispered firmly to Jimmy. Her soft, brown nude body hurrying in the candlelight mesmerized him. She piled his clothes and boots into his arms and shoved him through the tiny adobe out the back door.

Victor came, without invitation, walking through the front opening. Rosa finished pulling on her blouse, smiled, and curtsied to make him laugh, but he didn't. He looked out toward the back door and back to Rosa with a questioning, demanding look he asked. "¿Que era que?"

"Mi madre," she feigned.

Dejected, Jimmy sidled across the road to the hotel, avoiding Russ, with the intention to sleep through his dissatisfaction. In his room, Jimmy's frustration and disappointment showed in his eyes but no one could see. His passion boiled and urged him to defy Rosa's dismissal and return, but he didn't.

First thing in the morning the two cohorts, Jimmy on Darlin', and Russ on his horse, Willie, strolled over to the railroad depot. Jimmy felt nervous about this since he had only thirteen more dollars and two silver pesos left in his pocket. If he had to spend another three for the fare south and back, he would be cutting his finances close.

Russ struggled off his mount and said, "You hold the horses. I'll go in and fetch the tickets."

Walking back along the tracks up to Jimmy and standing between Willie and Darlin' his chest almost touching Jimmy's leg, Russ reached up and handed

Jimmy the train ticket. Jimmy had five silver dollars in his hand ready to drop into Russ's. Russ wouldn't open his hand to take them.

"Hey! You remember the time we rode the train to Stockton and you couldn't snatch that dern penny from my hand?"

"I remember. I couldn't keep Aunt Mary from snatchin' it from my hand neither. Bet I could snatch it now though."

"I bet you can't. Let's make it a twenty dollar bet!" Russ said.

"I ain't got twenty dollars, Russ! Let's just do 'er for fun," Jimmy replied.

"No way, José. Yer gona have to pay twenty to see my hand!"

"Well, I ain't got it!"

"Okay then, if I lose, you git one of my calves, and if you lose, you give me one of your calves."

"What calves?!"

"The Smokin'-T calves boy, where's yer brain!?"

They spent so much time arguing about the penny and the calves and the twenty dollars, they forgot to load up Willie and Darlin'. They had to run for it when the conductor yelled "Borrrt!" Fortunately, they loaded the horses and climbed aboard the train in the nick of time.

Sitting across from each other face-to-face, Jimmy set the Buntline next to him on the seat. He peered out the window in the direction of Cisco's Café hoping to get a glimpse of Rosa. Russ knew it. What Russ didn't know was that Jimmy's attention was also on Russ's goofy grin and the penny sitting in his outstretched flattened palm. Jimmy snatched it so quick, he could feel Russ's shock and dismay. Russ twitched his flat palm and flung it into a disconcerted fist.

"Now, that ain't fair. I weren't ready!" Russ whined.

Jimmy just grinned and kept looking out the window holding his trophy, tightly in his fist. Then, without looking at Russ, he relaxed his hand until it was almost flat, then quickly snapped it shut. Russ's bony fingers crashed into the knuckles of Jimmy's hand.

"So that's two calves you owe me, now." Jimmy grinned as he watched the wooden trestles over the Los Angeles River go by beneath the train.

Russ thought of complaining about not getting any warm ups. Or the bet was not valid because they never shook hands on it. Or some such nonsense, but that wasn't what he did. He just waited, letting his eyes lollygag out the window and slyly back to Jimmy's hand. This time when Jimmy's hand was completely flat and relaxed, Russ's was there and gone with the penny. Jimmy never even bothered to close his hand.

"No. That's one calf I owe you."

The two grown children played slap hands until Russ looked up and said, "That's The Pueblo de Santa Ana. There are some very wealthy families that live around these parts."

By then Russ owed Jimmy twenty-five head, more cattle than the Smokin'-T even owned.

"Well, how're we goin' to settle this little problem?"

"One more, double or noth...!"

Before Russ could finish the sentence, the penny vanished from his hand. "That's fifty head you owe me, Russ. You'll be dead before them twelve Smokin'-T cows ever give out that many calves!"

They laughed. The train rumbled into the heat of the wide canyon between the Santa Ana Mountains and the coastal Laguna hills. Jimmy dozed and rested his boots on the edge of the seat next to his companion.

"That beautiful place is the Mission San Juan Capistrano, home of the Juaneño Indians. They're related to the Gabrielinos back in Los Angeles, but they talk a little differ'nt."

Jimmy's head bounced and wobbled from side to side. He was sound asleep. Russ watched a group of the Juaneños, their dry skin tanned almost black from the heat and sun. They squatted under a sycamore tree, close to a cornfield, holding their primitive farm tools, watching Russ and the train rumble by. With blank eyes, a few of them slightly lifted their dangling hands into a paltry gesture of salutation.

The train left the canyon and the Juaneño farmers and the Mission San Juan Capistrano, jewel of the missions, and headed west for a few miles. Once at the shore the train veered left. Off to the right in view of the magnificent Pacific Ocean, breakers rolled, and more Juaneños frolicked in the surf.

These times in California were good times, easy times. Game was plentiful, the environment kind, and life was enjoyed by a lot of people.

Jimmy stirred when the train blasted its whistle. Slowly he opened his eyes. Five hundred yards away he saw the blue Pacific, contrasting against the lighter blue sky.

"We're here, boy," barked Russ.

"Oh" Jimmy yawned.

The compadres Russ and Jimmy, walked Darlin' and Willie down the ramp. Russ stayed up on the ramp and led Willie along side of it so he could step down into the saddle instead of climbing up. He just pulled Willie up close to the ramp, thinking he would step right on from above. But Willie didn't co-operate. Just as Russ stepped out, Willie sidestepped away, leaving Russ nowhere to go but down. It was a good thing he was paying attention. He leaped at the horse, catching the left stirrup with his right foot. Willie continued to spin backwards in circles. Russ now had his horse but couldn't go any farther, unless he wanted to mount up facing backward.

"Whoa, Willie! Damn you, whoa, you son of a bitch!"

The horse continued to step out in a direction it thought would get him away from the old Texan. Jimmy jumped on Darlin' loped up, circled Willie from the rear heading him off and forcing him up against the train cars, and to a stop.

Jimmy laughed so hard he could barely see. Russ pulled his right foot out of the stirrup and slid down Willie's side, resisting the urge to whip the belligerent brigand in the face. Willie lifted his nose and looked down it with fearful wide eyes in response to Russ's body language. Russ pulled hard on Willie's left rein spinning him in close, stepped into the stirrup and loped away.

Jimmy caught up and was still laughing. "Whoa, Willie, whoa!" He chortled.

Both Willie and Russ gave Jimmy cross but harmless looks. The road to the ranch headquarters wound east a couple of miles through rolling, grassy foothills. Cattle grazed everywhere.

"There must be thousands of head out here."

"Last count, old Doc said there was 25,233."

Approaching the magnificent ranch house, nobody

was in sight. Jimmy tied Darlin' to the hitching rail. Russ rode Willie around the house, through the back gate and right into the courtyard. Jimmy followed him on foot aware of the clacking noise Willie's shod hooves made on the tiled floor of the courtyard.

A Chinese lady with white hair came out, flour on her face and on her arms all the way up to her elbows. "Mister Russ! Get dat caballo out ' here, right now! He shit, you clean up!"

"Slow down, Showe Li, I'm goin', I'm goin'!"

Showe Li had cooked for the ranch for over forty years and appeared to Jimmy and most newcomers to be in charge of the entire place.

"Showe Li, this here's my amigo, Jimmy Longhon."

Showe Li eyed Jimmy's unusual gun-belt, scowled and turned toward the kitchen, "Doc at San Onofre corrals. You go der, he der late."

"Let's ride outa' here 'fore ol' Showe Li shoots one of us."

Russ and Jimmy backtracked to the rails and turned south along the Coast Road for about three miles. As they rode along, Russ told Jimmy about the Vaqueros. "You're going to meet the finest horsemen in California. They're a very private group, highly talented. They keep their trade secrets tight to their vest on the makin' of their leather tools. The craftsmanship in braiding rawhide riatas, reins, and saddles is an art. And the subtle way they use them is staggering. They make using those riatas look so easy. But let me tell you, it's very easy to snap one by pulling a little too fast or too tight. Their horses are trained to keep the tension just right as they pull in the animals. Their reputation of equestrian prowess and marksmanship is a well-cultivated legendary mystique on the Rancheros around here. It discourages any riff-raff that might wander into the area. All the way across the southwest, "Vaquero" implies a man of strength who deals out his own swift and lethal justice. The title Vaquero isn't used lightly. It designates a man as one not to be toyed with. So don't make 'em mad." Then Russ finished with one of his silly dodgy faces.

Russ and Jimmy road up to a small herd of steers milling around in a pen close to the railroad tracks. In the larger pens, three Vaqueros including Bibo, sat in their saddles. Bibo, the cutter and Doc's number two Vaquero, stood his horse in the gate blocking the cows. The other two riders roped calves by their back feet, dragged them away from their mothers over to the fire where two dismounted men castrated and branded them. A foul smell of burning hair drifted densely in the dusty air, and mingled with the yips and whistles of the working cowboys.

Doc and his man Ambrose sat mounted outside the corrals at San Onofre, watching the branding. Ambrosia Valenzuela, the head Vaquero was short, stocky and looked very much like Pancho Villa.

"Mira, Jefe, Russ has brought a companion with him." Ambrose leaned toward Russ and Jimmy.

The two men turned their horses' toward Jimmy and Russ as they rode up. Doc was expecting Russ, and didn't act surprised to see him with a companion.

"Russ, amigo, que pasa hombre?" Ambrose drawled.

"Russ! It's good to see you again,"

"Thank you, Doc, howdy, Ambrose. I'd like t' introduce young Jimmy Longhon from San Benito. Jimmy, this here's Mr. Doc O'Neill, owner of the Rancho Santa Margarita y Las Flores; one of the most thriving spreads and largest herd of cattle in Alta, California."

"I'm pleased to make your acquaintance, son. This is Ambrose Valenzuela my range boss."

"Saludos, Jaime, ¿Cómo está? " Ambrose reached out to shake Jimmy's hand. Jimmy responded cordially and shook hands with his new compañeros.

"I've got five fat steers cut out for you in this pen here Russ." Doc pointed casually towards the corrals.

Russ and Jimmy dismounted and strolled with Doc and Ambrose.

"It turns out I need more cattle than I mentioned in my letter." Russ disclosed quietly to Doc.

"Why's that?" Doc inquired.

Casually walking away and turning his back to Jimmy, "I owe the boy fifty head," Russ said quietly, "and I'd as soon settle up with 'im now while we're here and it's handy, rather than wait and have to deal with 'er later."

Doc glanced suspiciously at Jimmy. "What d'you have in mind Russ?"

"How 'bout them younglings you're working now? I'd take fifty heifers and bull calves t'day."

Doc looked at Russ suspiciously. "Those babies? You know better 'an that, Russ. Those calves are going to need six weeks, to be sure they don't come down sick from the branding. I have more than fifty little ones down by the Mission San Luis Rey you can take with you."

The Mission San Luis Rey lay seven miles to the southeast.

"We can ride down now, sleep at the mission, and drive the cattle back in the morning." Doc planned.

"Sounds good by me" Russ agreed. "How 'bout you, Jimmy?"

Jimmy grinned his consent, knowing he really had no choice and that Russ was just ribbing him as usual. Jimmy didn't hear Russ's comment to Doc, he didn't know Russ intended these fifty young calves for Jimmy and the Smokin'-T.

"Ambrose, have Bibo tell Showe Li and my wife that we won't be back until late tomorrow. Keep these five head for Russ penned here and be sure they're fed and watered"

Instructions given, the four mounted men headed southeast quartering away from the railroad tracks and the ocean.

Cattle appeared here and there, evenly spaced over the entire ranch. The day was temperate. If the sun were scorching, the cattle would have crowded into the scarce shade of the few live oaks that spotted the rolling hills.

"Hombres, mira allá." Ambrose pointed.

Still two miles away, the white buildings of the Mission San Luis Rey came into view from atop the rise. Green rows of cultivated gardens framed the bright, white Spanish buildings and walls. A lone priest hunched over in one of the rows. A herd of three hundred pound calves dotted the cleft between the rise and the mission.

"Since the calves are so close and right on our way, we may as well round 'em up now rather than chance them scattering in the night." Doc instructed.

"Sounds good to me." Russ replied, while winking and grinning at Jimmy.

The men spread out and started down the grade toward the cattle.

"Take it slow boys; we don't want that herd runnin' through the Padre's garden." Doc decreed.

The flighty calves eyed the infiltrators dubiously. Without lifting their heads, the calves tried to ignore the cowboys. While still cropping grass, they walked away sideways from the intruders. About then, Willie had an attack of some sort. The horse bolted ahead, looking behind himself at a mysterious assailant that nobody else could see.

"Whoa, Willie! Whoa, you son of a bitch!" Russ bellowed.

Then Russ understood the same message that Willie was responding to. He felt a burning pain on the knuckle of the middle finger on his right hand, then another on his right forearm. Yellow mud wasps were after Russ and Willie. Willie must have inadvertently stepped on their nest and the wasps were on the warpath. Russ swiped them away as fast as he could, but they only had to be near his skin for a moment to raise a fiery welt.

Swatting like crazy, Russ and Willie tore away from the scene, running for their lives. Doc, Ambrose, and Jimmy watched in amazement, perplexed as whether to laugh or take cover. None of the wasps came in their direction and Russ looked hilarious riding across the rolling hills, gesticulating, gyrating, and ducking from an unseen enemy. The men had no choice but to choke down laughs, and force their faces to appear concerned.

The calves paid close attention. At Willie's first violent scramble, the herd dodged like a school of fish in the opposite direction, directly toward the mission.

Ambrose and Jimmy loped away quick and wide, intending to circle around in front of the calves and save the Padre's garden. The three-hundred-pound calves couldn't run as fast as the horses and were easy to overtake. Once cut off, they didn't bother to charge off in the other direction. They milled together, tried to ignore the riders, and continued -- heads down, eyes up -- chewing grass.

Unorthodox but effective, the calf herding was complete. Ambrose stayed and quietly circled the group. Jimmy and Darlin' jogged over to check on Russ. The wasps stung him eight times. The worst was his middle finger on his right hand. The knuckle had swollen to twice its normal size.

Russ didn't think he was complaining, just explaining the situation to anyone who would listen, "The stubborn critters wouldn't give up, kept comin' at me, finally after 'bout a mile they let up. I can't believe how uncongenial and persistent the little fellers were!"

No worse for the adventure, Russ bounced back as usual. "I'll push, you and Ambrose hold the wings," Russ instructed.

The herd moved into the primitive corral made of sticks, wires, posts and rock, built against the back wall of the mission.

With all the cattle gathered into the corral, Ambrose on his fine horse, stood in the open gate.

"There ain't nothin' the matter with that calf," Jimmy

contradicted Russ's cull, "well, he might be a little skinny."

Inside the pen, Jimmy and Darlin' walked up behind the calves that Russ didn't want and pushed them towards the gate. Ambrose held back all the other calves and let the culls through. His horse, a well-trained cutter, was magnificent to watch. The cutting horse would spread his front legs and face off the calves that were not wanted to exit. If the calf persisted, the horse would jump to either side depending on which way the calf darted to block its escape.

The Padre of the mission, Father Martinez, wandered out to the corral. He was accustomed to Doc showing up without warning to use the facilities. The O'Niell's donated a generous tithe to keep the mission operating.

Father Martinez leaned against the corral fence with his arms folded on top. "Que pasa, Jéfe?"

Doc introduced the padre to Russ, "I'm sorry to barge in without notice, Padre. It was a last minute decision to round up these calves. We'll be out of your garden first thing in the morning." Doc and Russ and Father Martinez stood and watched until Ambrose and Jimmy had culled all the calves only penning the fifty Russ would buy.

Jimmy rode up to Russ, "Whoa! Willie!" He taunted him.

Russ's finger still painfully swollen, he gave Jimmy a childish evil grin.

The cowboys dined with Father Martinez on tortillas, beans, fruit and wine; prepared and served by Josephina, a seventy-year-old woman who lived at the mission. The wine was potent. Jimmy felt tipsy after one half of a mug. He fell fast asleep on the uncomfortable terra cotta tile floor after finishing the whole thing. The older men sat up late talking and playing cards.

At sun up, Jimmy opened his eyes. Josephina scooted by. The cowboys and Father Martinez were already sitting on the patio drinking coffee and eating tortillas wrapped around eggs, scrambled with onions and chilies.

"How're you goin' to finish them fifty head in Los Angeles?" Jimmy assumed Russ would have one of the local ranchers raise the cattle for meat for the hotel restaurant.

"These're your cattle, mister penny pincher." Russ reported.

"What are you talkin' 'bout? These ain't my calves. You bought 'em, Mr. Whoa Willie Whoa" Jimmy thought Russ was still teasing him.

"Listen ya little trail tramp, these calves 'ill settle our debt, so I don't have ta hear you belly achin' all the way back to the Pueblo 'bout ol' Russ welchin' on a bet." Russ knew Jimmy didn't complain about much, but he couldn't help teasing his naive friend.

Jimmy, almost speechless, said, "Now, dang it, Russ,

I can't take those calves, it ain't right and you know we weren't serious 'bout that bet."

"If I'd a-beat you, I'd be spectin' my calves, you sidewinder." Russ glared back at the boy.

Judging by the sound of his voice, Jimmy almost thought Russ was serious. Then Russ grinned his big, goofy, wrinkled grin and Jimmy relaxed. But he knew there would be no more arguing about it.

Ambrose and Jimmy ran the free roaming calves out of the area so they wouldn't join up with the fifty head in the corral. Then the four men started Russ's fifty. Quietly, so not to spook them, Doc and Russ rode into the corral on horseback. Jimmy and Ambrose waited on their mounts outside the fence, one on each side of the gate. They allowed the calves in front to get ahead; then they walked along side of them. Doc and Russ continued to push from the back of the group.

Fifty head was a small herd, but was still a dusty business. Jimmy felt guilty. He went back to spell Doc (never one to shirk a job) from the dust for a while, at the rear of the herd. It took seven hours to drive the calves back to the corrals at San Onofre and Jimmy ate plenty of dirt along the way.

Doc's wife, Alice O'Niell, a charming red haired woman with fiery eyes, was the stately matron of the Rancho Las Flores. She had Showe Li lay out a spread for the boys, bigger than Thanksgiving. She knew the meals at the mission were meager.

Alice knew old Russ very well and had no desire to hear too many of his stories. But this new young cowboy intrigued her. During the meal, she made a point to probe Jimmy about many aspects of his adolescent life.

"Tell me young man, why do you wear that rather large gun on your belt around with you all the time?" Alice inquired.

"I suppose, so's I've got it handy if I need it ma'm." Jimmy drawled respectfully.

"Now, what could you possibly *need it* for, Jim?" She mocked.

Unaware of her teasing, Jimmy replied seriously. "Well ol' Russ gave me the gun and I thought he'd like it if I wore it. I don't shoot it very often 'cept at practice. I reckon it doesn't have any real use other than makin' myself uncomfortable wearing it around all the time. Maybe bein' more accurate down range gives it a special use." Jimmy felt nervous and obliged to talk intelligently when speaking to the elegant lady.

Alice felt compelled to correct Jimmy's grammar but Russ interrupted, "This here boy's one hell of a shot, Mrs. O'Neill, and I taught him everything he knows." Naively, Jimmy felt shocked by Russ's proclamation. He was proud to be Russ's friend but the long demanding hours old Pots spent with him at the shooting range had paid off. Pots' friendship and lessons were very important to the boy. Jimmy attempted not to contradict Russ's participation in his training with guns. And Jimmy knew Russ was proud of him and found it difficult to spare his old pards feelings. "Almost everything," Jimmy asserted himself with an uneasy grin at the wrinkled old Texan.

After settling up in the morning, Doc said good-by to Russ and Jimmy from the ranch-house, "I've got guests coming in tomorrow Russ and some paper work to clean up. You boys'll find the corrals. Ambrose will help you get the cattle loaded."

Russ paid seven dollars a head for the grown steers and three fifty a head for Jimmy's fifty. "How much money 'v you got on you Jimmy?" Russ inquired as Willy and Darlin' dawdled down the road to the corrals.

"I don't know. Maybe thirteen dollars and some pesos; why?"

"After payin' off O'Niell, I'm broke until we get back to the pueblo." Russ knew his credit was good anywhere in the territory but explained it to Jimmy, anyway.

"How 'bout we drive the herd back to Los Angeles?" Jimmy queried.

"I don't think so amigo, you're talkin' at least seven days and maybe even two weeks. If they git spooked and brush up, we could loose half the herd. We'll line up somethin'," Russ returned.

Russ figured on getting some instant credit from the

train conductor. To Russ's surprise, the conductor was in a disagreeable state of mind. He told Russ he couldn't accept the cattle on board without payment in advance. This would have irritated the old Texan in his youth, but tired and fresh out of arguments, he said nothing.

Jimmy on the other hand told the conductor exactly how he felt about the railroad's policy. "Do you know who your talkin' to buddy? This here's Russ Tanner. He owns the biggest hotel in Los Ange…"

"Sonny, I don't care if he's Abraham Lincoln. I can't 'llow those calves on this train without payment --- in --- ad --- vance! So there."

"Well the Pacific Railway ain't go'na have any more of MY business!" Jimmy informed him. "As long as I live!"

"Well, I hope you have a long and happy life, Sonny." The conductor turned and stepped back onto the train car.

"What good is the stinkin' railroad if you can't use it when you really need it anyway?" Jimmy went on.

Russ and Jimmy had no other choice but to move the herd by hand, so to speak. Falling in behind and wide they took one last look toward the corrals and waved at Ambrose. From both sides of the herd, the two compadres began to gently whistle and yip. The calves looked up from their grazing disagreeably, and moved away from the harassment.

The young cattle had no idea what was happening. This driving business was all new to them. Fortunately, the five older steers fell into the lead and the young ones followed along.

A desolate narrow strip of land lay along the coast North, of the ranch house and south of the Mission San Juan Capistrano. There were steep hills to the east. In some cases, only a half-mile of land from steep bluffs to the vertical cliffs that went down to the ocean on the southwest.

Victor Machado, not a criminal by trade or habit, required all the money he could earn, to buy clothes that he felt would attract women and specifically Rosa. Now, rumor around the Pueblo talked of Rosa's feelings for the new gringo. Victor's jealous anger racked his every breath.

Through the dust, Russ and Jimmy at the rear of the herd simultaneously saw the silhouettes of horse-mounted men charging at the cattle. Then the cattle came to an abrupt stop in response to the gunfire of the intruders. The herd spun around and thundered away south toward San Onofre.

Jimmy drew his small Colt. Russ turned back to head off the stampede. Charging at the desperados, Jimmy held his fire to be certain he had a clear shot and double certain who he had a clear shot of. The two bandits had no time to reload and were not expecting retaliation from the old man and the gringo. They were fumbling with their empty pistols as Jimmy charged up on Darlin'. She tucked her hindquarters underneath herself. They came sliding up at full speed and Jimmy shot them both from twenty feet away.

Without looking back at his victims, Jimmy charged south to follow Russ. The gun battle in the distance urged him on but by the time he arrived it was too late. He recognized Victor's hat and black clothing and then Victor's face. Victor's horse had white froth all over its chest and neck. Victor warily circled east and wide of Jimmy away from the spot where Russ, Willie, and Victor's little brother Nicky lay dying in the dust.

Willy was down on his side. He tried to lift his head from the ground when he heard Jimmy ride up. But the good old horse couldn't muster the strength. He gave one last snort through his nose and lips, and then lay still. Russ and Nicky didn't move either.

Jimmy, stunned and quiet, leaned at first then squatted down and shook Russ -- but knew he wouldn't respond. And he didn't. Jimmy's mouth curled uncontrollably into a hideous frown. The pain in his throat was unbearable. He arched his back and lifted his face toward the sky. His vision still blurry, he felt the muscles in his lower lip relax. Then the same dark clouds as on the day he watched Cisco's funeral appeared. They looked like riders loping away across the sky over the ocean, out into the horizon. This time, however, he saw many more men on horseback loping off in a very long column. The same as Cisco described to Jimmy a long time ago riding along in Lupito's wagon. Were they in the dust or in the clouds? Jimmy would never know. Four hundred yards away, Victor sat on the side of the hill watching Jimmy muddling around. He knew the gringo would come for him, but not today.

Miguelle Lindo, a cattleman from Los Angeles, a close friend of Russ, and Doc's houseguest, rode up with Ambrose and Doc. They found Jimmy sitting in the dirt next to Willie's limp front legs. Amid the death, he senselessly gazed out over the ocean.

"When the herd ran into San Onofre we knew some trouble was up, but we didn't expect this." Doc said with quiet disdain.

"There's two more dead on the trail, up ahead." Jimmy said tonelessly. "Victor Machado was here, too. I'll be goin' after him," he said calmly, with a sadness so deep it made Ambrose turn and walk away. "Doc, could you keep my cattle down here for a while? I'll come back and drive 'em home, later."

Doc spent no time trying to talk Jimmy out of chasing down Victor. Who he assumed would be impossible for Jimmy to find. Jimmy rode back to the ranch house with Doc, Ambrose, Bibo and Miguelle to bury Russ.

"Ambrose, have Bibo ride up to the look out camp and watch the trails for Victor riding south." Doc sensed the rookie fugitive was smart enough to avoid any law enforcement to the north that would hear the news even if the train hadn't brought it.

Bibo rode into the ranch house two hours after dark with his report: "Victor rode south along the sand."

Jimmy's depression was so deep, he didn't say anything to Doc or Ambrose. He slipped away the next morning after the burial and road south.

Victor turned southeast along the Chula-Vista trail. Determined to stay on Victor's tracks, Jimmy interrogated all the travelers and residents along the way. Only eight hours behind on Victor's trail, Jimmy pressed on. Victor didn't believe the gringo would follow him so far south into Indian and Mexican territory. However, from high on the Yuma trail, Victor knew the lone rider far below was the gringo coming along, intent on finding and killing him.

Victor turned north and followed the hills into the Elsinore Valley then through Santa Ana and finally into Los Angeles.

Chapter Fourteen

In the twilight Victor leaned against the wall of the adobe where Rosa and her mother lived. His head bent talking through the blanket door. He glanced down the street to see Jimmy advancing. The tight hand of fear gripped his body. He cautiously backed into the street facing Jimmy. He had no idea what to expect. Jimmy, calm but completely insane, continued walking forward expecting Victor's lead to fly.

When Jimmy was still a hundred yards away, Victor pulled his pistol and began to fire. Before the hammer fell on Victor's first shot Jimmy had reached across his belt and pulled out the Buntline. Carefully, slowly, he took his best target stance and made a sight picture on Victor's chest. He heard the whine of Victor's bullets as they whizzed past his ears. In quick succession, almost overlapping, the last reports of the two boy's guns reverberated simultaneously. The Buntline lifted in Jimmy's hands from the recoil. Victor flipped back against the ground.

Rosa shrieked and ran down the street toward Jimmy. Her mother stood in front of Cisco's and silently choked back her weeping. "He won' stay lon'. She said to the waitress standing next to her on the boardwalk. "He will only brin' Rosa a life of sorrow. Belie'e me. I wanted to name her Dolores but I chose Rosa to spare her that sorrow."

Rosa had fallen deeply in love with the young gringo. Carmelita knew that young gringos never stay and never bring happiness to young, beautiful Mexican girls.

Rosa walked with Jimmy back to Darlin', who was hobbled on a little grass patch, just off the main street. They didn't speak. They were both in shock: Jimmy from the loss of his best friend, and Rosa, because of her release from the persistent Victor – and the gift of her guerta caballero, Jimmy Longhon.

That night, Jimmy against his better judgment went to Rosa's adobe and whispered her name through the wool blanket covering the doorway. Carmelita appeared in the opening, arms folded in anger. She sashayed out, and scolded Jimmy; "You're a murdering bastard! You'll burn in hell for eternity!" Even though she knew Victor wouldn't have made Rosa happy. She knew Victor would have been there every day for Rosa. That misery, she felt, was better than the loneliness brought by the absence of a wandering man.

Jimmy silently accepted Carmelita's scolding and walked away. Rosa caught up to him down the street and took his hand. Saying nothing to each other, they walked to the cienegas in the balmy night. A huge orange moon loitered in the summer sky. It back-lit the edges of wispy clouds stretched along the horizon, illuminating the trail to the river.

Preoccupied at first, both young souls thought nothing of their attraction to one another. The craving they shared for company emanated from a far simpler place. Void of wants, struggles, motives or outcomes, the two lonely hearts walked for hours along the river experiencing each other's silence.

Slowly, affection pressed against their fingers and

hands, urging Jimmy to test her consent to love. Bit by bit, molecule by molecule, Rosa silently agreed. She wanted his passion to trespass on her soft smooth brown skin. And trespass he did. In a violent dance of pleasure and pain, they rewarded one another with fulfillment of a magnitude unknown to the human experience. The satisfaction they attained transcended any previous spiritual or physical peak either had reached in life before. Or ever would again, no matter how hard they tried.

The sweat and dust from their struggle glimmered faintly on their bodies in the moonlight. Standing together they washed one another with the river lapping at their hips.

"Mi Corazon y amor es tuyo." Rosa whispered in Spanish. "I love you all my hear', Jaime."

He understood two words. Corazon and amore, enough to respond, "I love you too, Rosa, but I can't stay here in Los Angeles."

Fortunately for Jimmy, Rosa didn't understand him. She smiled and leaned her face against his wet chest.

Jimmy walked Rosa home. Hesitant to face Carmelita's wrath, he stood and watched Rosa enter her adobe from the boardwalk of the Hotel de Los Angeles. The smell of liquor, smoke, and kerosene fumes tainted the air exhaling through the saloon's louvered half-doors. Jimmy walked in. The din of the crowd softened. Every man turned, and a whisper spread across the room, "*That's* the boy who killed Victorito."

Drunk from overindulging in the distilled spirits of the mescal plant, Victor's father, Roberto Machado, staggered up to Jimmy. His companieros stood close behind. With crossed eyes, barely able to stand, with his index finger in Jimmy's face, the old man began to speak. "Whodju thin' you 're comin'to ma village n shoot my son? I to tisch ou lesson." Roberto couldn't see, stand, nor talk clearly. He cocked his arm and fist with an exaggerated motion and swung too heavily at Jimmy. Roberto's actions were abnormally slow and Jimmy easily stepped out of the way as Roberto, seized by his own momentum, stumbled forward and fell on the wooden floor.

Doc, Ambrose and Miguelle walked into the saloon just in time to see Roberto's fall, and the crowd of men concentrating on Jimmy in obvious support of Roberto.

"Hombres! Listen to me," Doc spoke up. "This boy has done nothing wrong. Victor and Nicky ambushed Russ and Jimmy on the Rancho Santa Margarita seven days ago and killed Old Russ. I talked to Rosa and Carmelita today. They told me Victor pulled his gun and began to shoot at Jimmy. Only then did Jimmy pull his revolver, amidst the storm of Victor's bullets, and shot to protect himself. You all know how much Carmelita loved Victor. She would rather burn in hell than make up a lie to protect this boy who killed him."

"The gringo boy deserves to die!" An invisible, pathetic voice yelled from the back of the room.

"Damn you, coward! Step up and state your business or shut up and get out! First of all, you're all standing in this boy's saloon. I talked to Alonzo Rodriguez, the attorney, this afternoon. Russ has no family and left all his holdings to Jimmy. And, second, if this boy is hurt in any way, Ambrose and Bibo, my Vaqueros, will hunt you down. They'll find every last one of you standing here tonight, and send you all to hell, whether you were involved or not. So it's your responsibility to keep this boy alive."

Doc would never have executed such a threat, but he had money that the men of the Pueblo knew of. The presence of Miguelle, Bibo, and Ambrose, three well-known Vaqueros, lent authority to Doc's ploy.

"I'm sorry for all this trouble, Doc. Russ did so much for me and everyone he knew. I don't know what to say," Jimmy apologized.

"I know, Jimmy. But look around. If you continue to take justice into your own hands, one day you'll have more justice than you can handle. We brought your cattle up on the train this afternoon. If you don't want them, I'll buy them back from you for the same price Russ paid," Doc said quietly and honestly.

"Thanks, Doc, but I'll keep 'em and drive 'em home. Russ wanted me to have 'em. I know he wants me t' make a go of the Smokin'-T, even if he ain't here to watch." Jimmy replied.

Inheriting the Hotel de Los Angeles, Cisco's Cafe and eighty thousand dollars took more time and energy than Jimmy could have imagined. Even understanding the wealth he had inherited was beyond Jimmy. Before Alonzo had completed all the paper work for Jimmy to sign, a month had gone by.

Jimmy spent every free moment with Rosa. They argued frequently, and then made peace in the one language they could both articulate. It was not always enough. There were times they couldn't find any way to resolve their quarrels. Rosa demanded that Jimmy leave her sight. She then found solace from Alonzo Rodriguez who articulated all of her fiery languages.

Carmelita reluctantly agreed to stay and cook at Cisco's Cafe. Alonzo agreed to manage the business, and accounting, for five percent of the gross. Alonzo also took sixteen thousand dollars, representing ten percent of the estate that Jimmy had inherited from Russ.

After his final meeting settling Russ's will, Jimmy went to visit Rosa at Cisco's; "I'm goin' to take the calves to San Benito. The land around the Pueblo is all taken and far too expensive to rent or buy for runnun' cattle on. The range is open east of San Benito where I can run the Smokin'-T cattle."

"Bastardo!" she sneered. "I'm pregnant, and now, you're leaving? My mother was right! Go! Leave! I will raise your child on my own!

That was the first Jimmy had heard of her condition, and it stunned him. “Are you sure?” He asked.

“Si! I am sure,” she scolded.

Jimmy had no idea of her tête-à-tête with Alonzo. “Rosa, I won’t go, at least for a while, at least ‘till the baby is born. I think we’ll make more money on these calves if they’re raised up north.”

Rosa grinned when Jimmy said we. “Are you to stay with me? You’re no’ angry?”

“How could I be angry at you? I love you so much. I can move into Russ’s place in the back of the hotel. Then we can get married …” Her expression cut off his words.

Rosa stiffened, “I don’ thin’ we shoul’ get marrie’ Jaime.” She said, utterly ignorant of how that simple statement devastated Jimmy. She didn’t realize her feelings would change later on.

“But Rosa, you’re going to have a baby, we should get married and make it right.” He begged.

“Maybe, Jaime, I don’ know. Don’ talk me abou’ it now.” She turned from him and crossed her arms.

Until now, he had successfully ignored his feelings for the girl he grew up with and always thought he would marry. Now he couldn’t ignore them any longer. He struggled with the pain of giving up Elsie and decided he had no choice. Rosa was going to have his child. There was nothing to do but accept the responsibility and marry Rosa. In his own mind, Jimmy detached himself from Elsie but neglected to inform Elsie of his decision.

Daily, during the months of her pregnancy, Rosa disagreeably complained, "Stay here with me for a while longer, Jaime. I'm too sick and lonely to stay in this little room by myself."

"I have to tend the herd, Rosa. You know Miguelle worries about the cattle getting into his corn, and if that happens, I'll have nowhere to keep them." Jimmy patiently explained.

Work with his cattle, decisions about the operation of the hotel, and dealing with Rosa, were difficult. Blindly moving through his life in an ignorant, unbalanced cloud Jimmy continued to think Rosa would marry him.

Rosa made heavy demands on Jimmy's emotions and time. He wanted Rosa to be happy, and their life to go smoothly. He bought her all the things that she asked for. Nothing seemed to make her happy. He kept quiet as her complaints increased in frequency and volume, proportionate to the size of her growing body.

When Jimmy was gone tending his cattle, Alonzo crept unseen through the back entrance of the hotel and visited with Rosa in Jimmy's apartment. She was heavy, but her youth aroused the older man in such a way that he couldn't think straight, nor control himself. She in turn enjoyed the attention given to her by such a powerful and attractive older gentleman.

Juanita Vermund, Miguelle's neighbor, raised and trained stock horses for the cattlemen. The Vaqueros called her La Doña Con Mucho Caballos (the lady with many horses). Juanita was a tall, stately woman with long, straight, gray hair and deep wrinkles on her face that reminded Jimmy of Russ. Her bright gray/blue eyes twinkled, as she spoke softly, with melodious, poetic expressions. She sounded as if constantly amazed by all facets of life. At the age of sixty, she still worked twelve hours every day with her herd.

Jimmy became friends with Juanita, because of her alluring way of engaging him in conversation. Also, because she was the best hand around, helping him with his cattle on Miguelle's land.

"There is no happiness, with Rosa, left in my life." Jimmy complained.

"Jimmy, you must know she'll never be happy. Stop trying so hard. Only she can make herself happy and only she knows what makes her happy." Juanita shared her deep and caring thoughts. Sadly, she knew of Alonzo's incursions but was too polite to tell Jimmy.

Chapter Fifteen
-1889-

When the child arrived, Jimmy attended to Rosa's every request. The tiny girl, Rosalita, was the apple blossom of his heart. Some nights the little girl couldn't sleep and fussed. So, bundled in Jimmy's arms, the two spent many hours walking around inside the hotel looking at pictures and interesting shapes on the walls in the middle of the night. Rosa rested well. With no reasonable explanation she continued to behave bitterly. She continually neglected herself and ultimately became undesirable to Jimmy.

Rosa didn't care. Alonzo still paid little visits while Jimmy worked his cattle.

However confused she was about her feeling toward Jimmy, Rosa loved Rosalita. Overwhelmed at times, Rosa gave all of her attention to Rosalita. However stern, she was still a good mother.

-1890-

The three of them continued along until Rosalita drew close to her first birthday. "Rosa!" Jimmy stormed in. "You're not going to believe this! A businessman from New York contacted Alonzo and wants to buy the hotel and cafe!"

He thought the news would make Rosa happy. They could travel and visit his family in San Benito.

"Jaime! You can't sell the business. We need that income!" Rosa insisted.

Speechless but bursting, Jimmy tried to hold back his explosion, but it finally erupted. "Damn you, Rosa! Damn you! I can't make you happy? Nothing I do is right! Nothing I do satisfies your nasty heart! I can't take this anymore, I'm going to take the herd north as soon as I can!"

He couldn't believe the sound of his own words. Once said, however, he understood the truth of them. Jimmy finally understood that these were the real feelings he had kept buried for the better part of two years.

Rosa became hysterical. "How can you say that? What about Rosalita? What will happen to her?" She attempted to manipulate him.

It no longer mattered to him. It was like someone had flicked a switch. "She'll be fine. I'll send money. Alonzo and Miguelle will make sure everything is okay."

He stooped under the low door and walked out of Carmelita's little adobe, up the street and into Alonzo's office. "Que Paso, Jaime? You don't look so good." Alonzo said nervously, always expecting Jimmy to find out and retaliate for his indiscretions.

"I'm not, Alonzo." Jimmy moaned. "Everything is over between Rosa and me. I can't put up with her one minute more. I've tried and tried and nothing I do is right. I'm going to take the cattle to San Benito. I need you to watch over things here."

"What about Rosalita? She will want her papa and will have a miserable life without him." Alonzo contested, but stopped himself when he realized the benefits he would gain if Jimmy left.

"Rosa will take care of her. She doesn't treat me like a husband. She won't marry me. She only wants money to support Rosalita and so that's what she'll have." Jimmy insisted.

"There is more than that, amigo," Alonzo said. "In time, you'll miss your daughter and the burning in your heart will never cease."

"I don't think so, Alonzo. I'm so sad and lonely right now; it couldn't possibly get worse." Jimmy grimaced at the results of his words.

"Do you want me to sell the hotel to the gentleman from New York?" Alonzo hoped.

"No. Run it. Run it, Alonzo, make sure there's enough money to take care of Rosa and Rosalita. I'll come back and to see you from time to time. Then we c'n decide about the hotel." Jimmy deliberated out loud.

Jimmy desperately missed Russ and wanted his advice at that moment, more than he'd ever wanted anything in his life. He lifted his hat from the top of the stuffed chair and walked out of the office into the bright sunny day, without a smile, without a handshake, the hurt deeper than any he had ever felt before.

Alonzo was relieved.

Jimmy arranged for Juanita, Miguelle and four other men to help him move the cattle to the depot. He remembered his threat to the conductor at San Onofre and worried if the conductor would remember as well. Once the cattle were penned up, they were easily loaded onto the train.

“Now you be careful out there in the great north west, young man.” Juanita told Jimmy.

“I will. You should come up to San Benito sometime and meet Whitey Whitmore. He could use a sweet young wife like you,” He joked, “to help him run the train depot at Coaling Station A.”

“Well thank you honey. You never know.” Juanita returned. “So long for now.”

“So long.”

Miguelle traveled with Jimmy on the train to Coaling Station-A. The coaling station had grown. Now several homes lined a street that ran perpendicular to the tracks. A livery stable and general store stood connected to the supply warehouse and the large white letters on the water tank now read Coalinga.
“Howdy, Whitey.”

Without looking up Whitey spoke, “Hold on a stitch. I’ve got t’ figure out this bill o’ lading; I’ll be right with . . . Well for goodness sakes, if it ain’t the Scourge of the West. We thought you’d fallen off and was never comin’ back.”

“Ah, come on, Whitey. You knowed Russ got kill’t and left me all his stuff. It took forever to sort out all the business. But I’m back now. What ‘d you do, invite all your relatives t' come and live at the depot and change the name of the place?"

"How 'bout that? Little old Coaling Station A is now an official township, Coalinga, California. And you're right, the population, with all the open cattle graze, we surged from one, yours truly, to nineteen." Whitey pointed out. "This here's a thriving metrofolus."

"Yep, even with the crowds around here, it's still more relaxing, and comfortable than the Big Pueblo. Just seeing your ugly, old mug is a sanctuary for me."

"You don't have to get all vicious, Jimmy. Just 'cause you're the Darling, Scourge of the West, cowboy from the Big Pueblo."

Jimmy was happy to be home. He looked forward to seeing the rest of his old friends in San Benito.

One more undertaking needed to be completed before Jimmy could ride the rest of the way home. Miguelle helped him drive the cattle west until they saw the first range cow with a Smokin'-T brand. Jimmy and Darlin' sauntered over to Miguelle. "Amigo, muchas gracias. I can't tell you how grateful I am for all the help you've given me with the cattle and Rosa and Rosalita. I'll miss you, Miguelle. Here's some money. I'll be headin' into San Benito now and leaving the cattle to graze here."

Miguelle declined the envelope. "I won't take your

money, Jaime. Someday, I'll need a favor from you and you'll find me knocking at your door, don't turn me away. Remember, when you're in The Pueblo, you'll always have a room in our house. Adios, Jaime, vaya con Dios." With that, Miguelle and Jimmy split their trail.

Chapter Sixteen

"Ma!"

Jimmy's mother had an orphaned calf in the barn and was attempting to train it to drink out of a bucket. "Oh, my!" She whispered, hurrying to get up. "A'm out back honey!" She shouted. "Oh dear!" She whispered, and ran out to find her son. "Oh, Jimmy, you're home, you're finally home! You look grand!"

"You, too, Ma!" He hugged his mother tight.

"I have to go over to Shorty's. He's fixin' a tire on the wagon. Let's go surprise him!"

As they walked through town, Jimmy asked, "Have you seen Elsie?"

"She's busy, Jimmy."

"What d'ya mean, busy?" Jimmy persisted.

"You just got here. Let's go see Shorty. He'll be so happy to see you."

"Come on, Ma. What's up? What are you trying to keep from me?"

"Well now, Jimmy, you just got here and I don't want you upset but Elsie is engaged to be married." Jimmy's mother tried to calmly explain.

"To who?" He asked quietly.

"I don't want you to get upset, so let's talk about this tomorrow."

She didn't have to say anymore. Only one person engaged to Elsie could upset him more than the fact itself. He tried not to let it bother him. Shorty stood up from the wagon when he heard footsteps scraping on the dirt floor of the old blacksmith shop.

"Well, A'll be, look who's back!" Shorty grinned.

Shorty walked up, resisting the urge to ruffle Jimmy's hair. Jimmy reached with his right hand and took him in a grip that would have been difficult to escape. Then he pulled him up close and wrapped his left arm around his shoulders and squeezed him tightly like Russ had done to him two years earlier.

"Ah believe this is the first time ah've ever seen that boy give another man a hug." Dora said. Everybody had watery eyes.

"I brought home fifty head of cattle." Jimmy grinned at his mother, wiggling his eyebrows over Shorty's shoulder.

"I certainly hope they're not makin' a wreck of the house." Shorty chortled.

Dora Longhon was very proud and happy her son was back and invited everybody in town to supper that night. Lolo killed and plucked three fat chickens. Mrs. Miller made a lemon upside down cake that she baked in a huge cast iron skillet, made with fresh lemons from the tiny lemon tree growing next to her back porch. Shorty brought a jug of home made root beer that tasted heavily of yeast. But, after hanging in the well all morning, its cold, sweet fizz refreshed everyone who tried it. Ohma and Gunther brought sauerkraut and brat wurst. Mr. and Mrs. Cutchel brought Elsie.

"Hey, Jimmy." She smiled and ducked her head sideways shyly, the same way she did the day before he left.

"Hey, Elsie." Jimmy whispered. "I've missed you."

"Well, tell us about your adventures," Everyone insisted. Nervous at first, Jimmy started in. Pretty soon the nervous feeling went away. He didn't leave out the tiniest detail, from Whitey still referring to him as the Scourge of the West that morning to the pain of sleeping on the terra cotta floor at the Mission San Louis Rey. And everything in between, with one exception -- he carefully left out the slightest hint of Rosa and Rosalita.

When Jimmy got to the part about Juanita Vermond's ramuda, Jimmy's mom cut in, "Just what is a ramuda?"

"It's a herd of horses." Shorty tried to elaborate but was quickly cut off by Whitey. "Let the boy tell us his stories."

The skin on his face a little leathery, hair turning sandy in color, Jimmy glowed from his travels and the attention his friends bestowed upon him. In the eyes of his neighbors, Jimmy seemed a hero and drew a great deal of attention.

"I can't remember any young man Jimmy's age ever leaving San Benito for two years then coming back with such marvelous stories of adventure." Nobody could and Elsie looked upon Jimmy from an entirely new perspective, with echoes of old desires.

Here's a man of adventure and travel who she trusted and loved and dearly missed. Elsie thought of having Jimmy back. Maybe he would run away with her, so she wouldn't have to tell Walt. She wanted life the way it was before Jimmy had gone to the Pueblo.

"Will you walk me home, Jimmy?" Elsie asked at the end of the evening as the rest were saying good-bye.

Jimmy dearly wanted to walk along the dim streets of San Benito to Elsie's house, maybe stop in the deep shadow of the livery barn. But he felt she wasn't his any longer. Being the respectful guy he was, it didn't seem right for him to intrude on a life that he was no longer part of.

"Well, I'd like to, Elsie, but ain't there somebody around who wouldn't take too kindly to that?" He asked.

"Jimmy Longhon! You know what I mean!" She said. Then she whispered so no one else could here, "You never let something like that stop you, before."

"Not tonight, Elsie." He smiled sadly.

He expected her to run to Walt to satisfy the desires stimulated by him. He misconstrued them as frivolous whims, when in reality they originated in the deepest reaches of Elsie's heart.

Elsie left with her parents, perplexed by Jimmy's attitude. She misinterpreted Jimmy's sadness, sense of honesty and fair play, as big city snobbishness. She couldn't have been more mistaken. Their love for one another had grown deep and rich in their young callow hearts, but neither had the insight or tenacity to quarrel about it.

Jimmy spent the next two weeks with Aaron, counting, branding, culling and shipping the Smokin'-T cattle. In a makeshift corral, the boys sorted out six head they would trail to Coalinga and ship to market. "Aaron, you did a perty good job on these cows f'r the last two years."

"I reckon so, for a one man outfit, working once a month for two years." Aaron returned.

After losses, including the widow Millers old cow, and adding fifty head from Russ, and culls, the Smokin'-T had eighty head on the range.

The west bank of Dust Creek marked the border

between the Freye Ranch and railroad land. The Railroad land was for all intents and purposes open range and included all the land up to the railroad tracks and ten miles beyond to the central valley trail. The Freyes had more land on their side than they could use for the number of cattle they owned. Several small outfits, around the same size as Jimmy's herd, ran cattle on the Railroad's side of the creek. From time to time the small outfits would get together to cut out the Freye's stock and drive their herds back across the creek, onto the railroad land.

With the livestock work complete except for shipping, Jimmy began to think. He deeply missed Elsie. He thought if he lived outside of town he wouldn't think about her as much. He felt life would be easier and quieter out by the cattle. The railroad's tract of land was not for sale and the Freyes, he felt, were unapproachable to purchase land, "Aaron, if I was old Walt, I wouldn't sell a tiny chunk of land to me just to build a house on, would I?"

"I think you're right. Maybe the railroad would let you build a line shack or somethin' like that." Aaron speculated as they rode along.

The forty-two dollars received from the cattle buyer in Coalinga all went to Aaron for two years' wages, not bad for the times and hours spent actually working.

In Coalinga, after shipping the steers, Aaron and Jimmy ran into Little Walt. He didn't recognize Jimmy at first. Then taking a second look, he relaxed into a cocky posture. “So, you’re back. Elsie told me and now I see it with my own eyes. I thought I’d chased you out of these parts. And I’d never see you again.”

“Walt, you couldn’t scare a cat out of a dog house.” Aaron broke in.

“Come on, Aaron.” Jimmy turned to walk away.

“You’re still runnin’, hey Long Gun, well, that’s good -- stay out of my way.” Walt had an irritating way about him that could spell death in the west.

Pausing, Jimmy spoke. He didn’t bother to turn, nor look Walt in the eye. Over his shoulder, nonchalantly, gazing down the road he said, “Walt, you’re goin’ t’ mouth off t’ the wrong hombre and lose a few teeth or maybe your life, one of these days.” Jimmy tried to be subtle. “I hope you’ve kept up on your target practice with that dented old gold Colt of your fathers.” He knew the gun wouldn’t have been reparable after the thrashing he gave it.

The sinewy look of the weathered young cowboy, the deadly appearance of his saddle-worn guns and the solid reputation Jimmy had inadvertently earned as a gun fighter frightened Little Walt, who, despite his belligerent mouth and attitude, was not a complete moron.

Little Walt had also noted the subtle change in his fiancée as she relayed the adventures of her dear old friend.

Little Walt hadn't felt the necessity to carry a side arm. His German Drilling stylishly decorated the fine leather sheath under the left stirrup strap of his saddle.

Continuing to walk away, Jimmy looked at Aaron, "Little Walt sure won't be agreeable to me settling out east of Dust Creek or selling me some land. He hates me so much, I'm surprised his father still trades calves with us."

Little Walt was so jealous of Jimmy he really did hate him more than he realized. Walt Senior hoped that his son would somehow gather the courage to become a productive member of the Freye family. Walt Senior connected that hope with the marriage of his son to Elsie. He knew she worked hard, and was a sensible young lady with strong family values.

"Longhon is so damn self confident. I hate him. He irritates me." Little Walt confided in Whitey standing in front of the railroad agent's desk in hope of support.

A true coward and just not a good person Little Walt's self-absorbed thoughts leaked out, "I'd snuff Longhon if I wouldn't get hung."

"You're mistaken, Walt," the railroad agent replied, "I've never met a boy less full of himself, with more reason to be, than Jimmy Longhon. The boy's had a tough life, but still keeps his nose to the grindstone and works hard every day. I understand he don't even have to work. With the money ol' Russ left him, he could sit back and do diddly and live just fine, 'n he don't. He works his ramuda. Keeps up on his cattle and helps his ma around her place."

"Ah, big deal," Little Walt didn't get it, "My family's got a hundred times the money that hay seed's got. He'll regret he ever came back around these parts."

In a jealous rage, Little Walt rode off toward home all bothered about Jimmy and Aaron.

The locals laughed at Little Walt's abusive actions. Friends were hard for him to come by. He pressed too hard on people and even pressed too hard on his horses. He pressed too hard on everything and everybody, except Elsie.

Mindlessly persistent, his horses got their revenge in the end by jarring his teeth out whenever he wanted to ride anywhere. He didn't have the knowledge or patience to train his horses to jog along nice and smooth and anticipate his wishes. They were very nervous and worried about when they would get slapped in the face again during one of Walt's tantrums.

After leaving the depot, Little Walt headed along the trail home, ahead of Aaron and Jimmy. A few miles out of Coalinga, he decided to give Jimmy another scare. Walt waited, sitting in the dark shade of an Oak tree overlooking the shallow valley. The German Drilling rifle rested on his lap across the saddletree. His horse fidgeted. It didn't feel like waiting to find out what Walt had in mind.

When Little Walt saw Jimmy and Aaron turn the bend

into sight he lifted his gun, aimed carefully at the trail, well behind them and squeezed the trigger. With a loud *Kablam weeeen* -- the bullet ricocheted into the distance. Little Walt's horse responded to the gun blast instantly. It leapt straight up. The powerful, violently frightened animal scraped Walt's face, shoulders, and chest against the tree limbs, knocking him out of the saddle. Unfortunately his foot slid through the stirrup and hooked. The horse didn't stop. It dragged and kicked Walt into a bloody pulp. Jimmy and Aaron rode up, settled the horse, and unhooked Walt's shattered leg from the saddle.

"He was shootin' at us, y'know." Aaron said flatly.

"I know, Aaron, but djeeze, look at him. I don't know what we can do. He won't be able to sit up in the saddle even if he wakes up. When he does wake up, he's goin' t' be in some real bad pain. Lets lay him over his saddle. You take him on to his place goin' real slow. I'll ride ahead faster int' San Benito and fetch Lolo and Shorty and anyone else who c'n help." Jimmy grimaced at the sight of Walt as he spoke.

After carefully loading Walt on the antsy horse, the boys parted. "See ya out there, Jimmy." Aaron said.

Inadvertently, the jostling Walt received on the horse helped save his life. When Walt stopped breathing the jostling pumped air back into him and got his breathing started again. When Walt's heart stiffened up, the jostling brought him back again. All the time Aaron rode along, unaware of how serious Walt's condition actually was.

The hands at the Freye Ranch came out when they saw Aaron riding up.

"His horse 's done trashed him good. Jimmy and me come up and unhooked his leg but I think its perty bad." Aaron called.

Walt Senior came out. "Did you boys see what spooked the horse?"

"Well, he was shootin' at somethin' while settin' in the saddle up under an oak tree and the horse went crazy under the tree n' now, well, here we are."

Three hours later, when Lolo, Jimmy, and Shorty came riding in, Little Walt was still unconscious in his bed. Aaron and Jimmy were amazed at the pristine ranch house. Walt's pant leg was cut open. A shard of sharp white bone protruded through the skin on his shin. Those who looked, couldn't keep from cringing at the sight.

Little Walt's mother sat in the drawing room sobbing, while Dora Longhon tried to console her. "Oh, my dear, now, Mrs. Freye, try not to cry. Your boy'll come 'round."

Elsie stood with her arms folded, leaning against the wall next to Walt Senior. Lolo and Shorty examined Little Walt and discussed what to do.

"We don' even to'ch heem, jus' cart de boy ou' to de depot ándele an' take heem to Stockton or San Francisco." Lolo insisted.

"You're right." Shorty agreed. "We could try 'n put that leg back together but we might cut or sew the wrong thing and the boy could be deformed or even die. It's a miracle he hasn't bled to death as it is."

"That's what we'll do then." Walt Senior decided. "Come on, boys, let's load him in the buckboard and get goin'."

Lolo rode, cushioning Little Walt's head, in the wagon with Walt Senior. Jimmy rode along with the wagon on horseback. Aaron, Shorty, and the Freye's Ranch hand rushed ahead to make any arrangements they could at the depot. The boys knew better than to lope a horse the full six miles into Coalinga. So they loped and walked and trotted and walked and rushed the animals as much as they could without killing them. All three horses had a white, foamy lather of sweat covering their chest and shoulders when they skidded up to the depot.

"Whitey, when's the next train goin' north? Young Walter Freye's done hurt himself up real bad." Shorty burst out.

"It ain't 'till tomorrow sometime. What's happened?" Whitey probed with sincere concern.

"Little Walt's horse went crazy on him. Walt hooked his leg in the stirrup and got thrashed damn near to death. The boy's leg's got a big ol' hunk o' bone stickin' out! Not to mention he's black 'n blue 'n bloody 'n swollen all over!" Shorty reported with wide, nervous eyes.

Whitey went directly to the telegraph key and started clicking away. After fifteen minutes, he read his scratching to the boys. "Doc Segul stop San Francisco Memorial Hospital stop taking next train south stop mix syrup and water drip into victim's mouth every few minutes stop. Looks like we're t' keep Little Walt warm and comfortable."

At eleven thirty that night, the South bound train's whistle hooted its approach to Coalinga. The boys waited anxiously for the doctor. Little Walt, still out cold, wrapped in blankets, slept lying across tables in the depot.

Accompanied by another doctor and two nuns, Dr. Segul stepped off the train and was then surrounded by Walt Senior and his worried companions. "I'm Dr. Segul. Let's have a look at the boy," The doctor ordered.

"I'm Walter Freye, Little Walt's father; he's the boy who's been hurt."

"Fine, fine, let me in here."

After examining Little Walt for a while the, doctor said; "yes, yes, I've seen worse, but not much when still livin'. We'll have to take him into San Francisco. Putting this back together won't be easy and damn near impossible here. The boy seems stable right now. Hopefully that won't change between now and tomorrow night."

The North bound arrived the following morning at

eleven thirty. Walt senior and company gingerly loaded Little Walt into the train car. Walt senior left with Dr. Segul's group on the train north.

Then, with the excitement over, Jimmy and Aaron felt as if their feet were still moving and there was no place to go. The group rode away together, feeling the strong camaraderie from helping in the emergency that consumed their emotions and energy for the last twenty-four hours. They rode their horses tightly side by side, a few in front, a few behind, all wanting to stay in close to hear the conversation of old war wounds and theories of what Little Walt was up to.

"He was trying to bushwhack Jimmy and me." Aaron said in disgust, not happy in general about Little Walt's relationship with Elsie.

"He was just tryin' to scare us Aaron. If he'd wanted to, he could have shot either of us or either of our horses, as close as we were to that German long gun he's got." Jimmy interrupted.

"There's the oak he was under." Aaron pointed out.

Jimmy left the group of riders, loped up to the tree, and swung off Darlin'. The Drilling lay in the middle of the moist freshly scraped up grass and dirt where Walt's horse had pawed the ground. He jumped back on Darlin', carrying the rifle, and caught up with his companions. "Little Walt's going to have to ask me for this piece back in person and explain himself, before I return it to him." He said adjusting the German gun to balance on his legs.

"That seems fair." Everyone agreed except the Freyes' ranch hand. "Don't ya'll think since he's hurt he ought to have a little consid'ration?" He inquired.

Even though he felt the bond of the group, he also felt his loyalty to the Freyes. "Guess not." He answered himself.

"Little Walt has got to get some sense in his head if he survives this one." Shorty imparted.

"Jyes!" Lolo agreed. "He can not go on da way he has been. If dees one don't keel heem; who kno's what he might try next time?"

Lolo didn't say anything more, just listened to the banter and the squeaking saddles. They jostled along the trail, the horses at a slow walk. At the fork in the trail onto the road leading to the Freye's ranch house, everyone turned together. The news of Little Walt and his father going to San Francisco hadn't reached the Freye's Ranch. Elsie and Dora Longhon needed escorts back to San Benito.

Chapter Seventeen

In San Francisco, Little Walt received the best medical care money could buy. The nuns wrapped bandages, wet with Epsom salts, around his leg every hour during the day to ward off infection in his surgical wound. At night, the stitched wound dried without covering in the open air. The excruciating pain became dull with the use of opiates, but the dosage had to be increased every few days to maintain the drug's effectiveness. As a result, the boy became addicted. When the time came for Little Walt to get out of bed after seven weeks of horizontal bed rest and painkillers, his head was spinning.

"He'll have to go through the withdrawals then, if that's what it takes." Walt Senior told Dr. Segul.

Even though his leg had mended to the point he could start to walk again, the poor boy spent two more weeks, drawn, fevered, throwing up and begging for just a little relief, but given none. Walt Senior sat and watched his son in agony worse than the original accident. He held him and wiped with wet cloths to cool and sooth him. But forced him to face the pain involved in ridding himself of the morphine that he pleaded for.

Dr. Segul came into the room to see a sad young man sitting up in bed slowly consuming his breakfast. "Good morning Walt -- Mr. Freye. I'm glad to see you're eating. You have a lot to be thankful for, young man. If your friends hadn't come along and brought you home and then to the depot, you wouldn't be with us right now."

Little Walt said nothing, just stared over his bed tray at the doctor. His eyes looked sleepy with wide, yellow bags under them. His left eye drooped and his upper lip on the left side had been cut away by the horse's hoof and had healed, leaving his upper teeth exposed on that side. Seriously deformed, his leg still functioned, but he walked with a rolling limp. He couldn't have been less happy, nor would he accept the responsibility for his actions. His hate for Jimmy smoldered in the recesses of his soul.

Chapter Eighteen

Elsie waited nervously with her family and friends in the bright mid day sun at the depot for Little Walt's train. Jimmy had avoided Elsie ever since the accident, feeling his unfair advantage even though his feelings for her were very strong. Elsie had been extremely disappointed in Little Walt's behavior, but felt obligated to support him through his rehabilitation. But her thoughts were always wondering about her true partner, Jimmy.

Very conflicted, Elsie stood with Mrs. Freye. Elsie was stunning. She wore a brand new yellow dress, with wide white ribbons, that she'd made with her mother's help. Looking far down the track, they watched the train's whistle blow out a huge, white, plume of steam, and a moment later they heard its whistle hoot. Elsie's heart beat heavily, and she had difficulty catching her breath. Walt hadn't answered any of Elsie's letters and the only news she'd received was from Walt Senior through his wife.

The train rumbled in slowly and scratched to a stop. The engineer leaned out of the engine window. He grabbed the valve cord and gave Elsie a big grin, then blasted the whistle long and loud. She glanced down, embarrassed. Her mouth slightly open, her forehead wrinkled with the hesitation of seeing Little Walt. Elsie's heart pounded ever harder. Her conflict was so strong that she really didn't know her true feelings. She waited in the expectant crowd for her intended.

As the entourage disembarked, a bent little man that Elsie didn't recognize limped to the Pullman door and hesitated. His ascot crooked, his clothing too large for his skinny frame. His left eye and lip deformed, he looked out from under the derby hat with sad apprehension surveying the crowd for Elsie.

Elsie's joyful but strained face fought with her heart. She forced the smiling expression she wanted and felt was expected of her. The corners of her mouth couldn't support the weight of her sorrow and disappointment that pulled the smile down into a worried frown. She tried, but she couldn't look Little Walt in the eyes. Her gaze kept staring at his lip. He noticed her trouble and shoved her aside rudely and limped awkwardly away. "I don't need your pity!"

Her lower lip quivered upward over her teeth. She felt a surge of uncontrollable pain in her wet eyes and heart. No longer able to look at Little Walt, she turned and ran down the boardwalk, climbed into her family's buckboard and drove away, sobbing.

"I want to ride back to the ranch alone." Little Walt said to his parents. The horse from the accident had been given its own rehabilitation to school it from ever hurting another rider. They had tethered it to the wagon on the trip to the depot, feeling it would be good for Little Walt to get back in the saddle.

Out with his cattle Jimmy saw the Cutchel's

buckboard with Elsie driving along the trail. He rode up to see why she was alone.

At the crossing of Dust Creek, Little Walt saw the Cutchel's mule hobbled close to the wagon, chewing grass. Walt turned north, riding slowly along the water's edge. Rounding a bend, he was hidden under the cover of a dense growth of cottonwood trees. The afternoon sun sparkled through the leaves. The light played in the glen. The day was quiet and pleasant. He stopped and surreptitiously watched and listened to the couple.

Elsie and Jimmy sat close to each other at the top of a thirty-foot bluff that jutted out forming a peninsula. Elsie told Jimmy about the events at the depot and her doubts about Little Walt. They could see the creek on both sides. The moving water made a hairpin turn. Close to the edge of the bluff grew one very tall lone pine. The pine was the reason the bluff was there. Its roots held the ground together causing the creek to erode far away and around the tree forming the point of land overlooking the creek.

"Will you marry me, Elsie? I've been thinking about you ever since I've been home. Until hearing what you've just told me, I thought you loved Walt and wanted him." Jimmy explained gently.

I do love Walt, Jimmy. But I've always loved you and waited and waited, and then thought you'd never come home." She replied.

Walt looked down at the empty rifle sheath under his

leg. Something about the pleasantly warm, quiet beauty of the day, something about the horse's bent necks cropping grass, something about his miserable existence touched his soul that day. He turned back into the cottonwoods, never seen by Jimmy and Elsie. He told his parents about the two and that Jimmy had gone behind his back and proposed.

Jimmy didn't look at her. Instead he looked out over the creek and the expanse of wild barley. "Remember when we used to lie in the tall green barley and hold hands and look at the sky?"

"I remember it, Jimmy. I wanted to marry you then. I don't know if my folks would have let me." She gazed off in the same direction as Jimmy.

"So, if you still love Walt, what 're you goin' t' do?" He asked.

Grinning mischievously she leaned her face very close to his. She looked him closely in the eyes. She brushed his lips with hers and spoke in a throaty whisper, "I'm going to marry you."

-1891-

Walt Senior secretly spent the next six months surveying and working on a deed for a little point of land along Dust Creek.

"I'm not going to attend that hay seed wedding." Little Walt informed his parents. "I don't agree with you giving them that piece of land either!" He was steaming with jealousy and disgust.

Elsie wore honest white to her wedding in the little chapel in San Benito. Everyone in San Benito, Coalinga, and the surrounding area attended with one exception.

Weddings in the rural west and small towns were the single most exciting and sought after social events of the year. Guests sojourned for days just for a little cake, a lot of food, a little distilled spirit, and a lot of hijinks and dancing.

Elsie glowed in her grandmother's wedding dress. Her father ordered a new suit of clothing from the Sears and Roebuck catalogue, as did Jimmy, Aaron, Whitey, and Shorty. Sears, a new store out of Chicago, would send just about anything imaginable across the country through the mail.

Walt Senior and his wife came up to the wedding couple during the dancing and handed a large stiff parchment envelope and to Elsie. "This is from us, dear." Mrs. Freye said to Elsie. "And thank you from the deepest corners of our hearts, Jimmy, for helping Little Walt that day, when he so little deserved it."

The envelope contained a deed and right of way easement. The legal description defined a point of land that overlooked Dust Creek, three quarters of a mile north of the Coalinga trail crossing. Surrounded by twenty acres of land, the point would be known from that day forth as Longhon Pine.

The Freyes slipped away from the wedding after that, and couldn't be found to thank for the generous gift. Elsie and Jimmy knew exactly where the described land was. They couldn't, however, figure out how the Freyes knew the spot where Jimmy proposed to Elsie.

Two hundred riders and twenty-eight wagons followed the couple's bumpy ride in the Longhon's wagon to the depot from San Benito. Many of the riders followed the train out of Coalinga for so long that Elsie began to worry. "Do you think they're going to lope those horses all the way to San Francisco?" She asked seriously.

The couple honeymooned in San Francisco for three weeks at the Palace Hotel. Jimmy remembered it from Russ's stories. Elsie became pregnant on her wedding night and knew it. She loved Jimmy with all her heart and couldn't have been any happier. Jimmy felt loved, and returned her gestures ten fold. He couldn't do or say anything that he thought might hurt or upset Elsie, and she acted the same toward him.

They spent their time rambling around San Francisco by trolley, streetcar and on foot. They attended the theater, the ballet, and the symphony, and found the pawnshop where Russ had bought Jimmy's Buntline. Jimmy fell deep into thought at the pawnshop as he contemplated his life. "Russ walked through these very same doors the same as us, eight years ago. He was thinking about me then and here I am thinking about him."

"Do you miss him, honey?" Elsie squeezed his hand and felt his melancholy mood.

"Yes. I miss him everyday, Elsie. I miss Cisco, even though I can barely remember what he looked like. I miss Pots, and I'm thankful he taught me to shoot, or I might not even be here right now." Jimmy caught himself before he said anything about Victor or Rosa or Rosalita. Elsie thought nothing of what Jimmy said and allowed him his silence. She had a deep sense of respect for his privacy.

The two lovers strolled aimlessly in the city of the gay nineties. "Let's go in here and see what Can-Can shows are, Okay?" Jimmy asked innocently. Equally ignorant of what to expect, Elsie agreed.

They both sat, embarrassed, once the legs and skirts began to fly. "Oh my gosh! I didn't expect that," Elsie whispered. They left a little ashamed but undeniably tantalized by the end of the show. "I don't know what to say," she worried a little giggle to Jimmy, ducked her head sideways and shrugged her shoulders.

"You don't need to say anything, Elsie. Maybe you need to lie down for a little nap back at the hotel." Jimmy carefully concealed his arousal. When she ducked her head sideways, the way she had a habit of doing, it stimulated Jimmy's oldest, fondest memories of her.

Long Gun

Chapter Nineteen

Immediately upon returning from their honeymoon, Jimmy began work on their home at Longhon Pine. The land laid flat on the little mesa that spread away from the creek. Leveling the ground was not necessary. Jimmy ordered a prefabricated Victorian house from a catalogue Elsie had been saving and dreaming over for three years.

Aaron, Elsie, Shorty, Lolo, and a crowd of friends waited at the depot anxiously socializing. The mail order home arrived at Coalinga aboard a huge, flat, railroad car. The men had prepared to move the units of numbered lumber by building an assortment of riggings, such as A frames, wheels, axles, fulcrums and levers.

Heavy timbers placed against the flat car acted as a ramp. The crowd of men pulling on ropes, threaded through the top of the A-frame and tied to the huge stacks of lumber, started the lumber sliding down the timber ramp to the gravely ground along the railroad tracks.

Lolo stood on top of an adjacent unit of lumber up on the flatcar. "Hol' on tigh', boys! She's going to cöme har' now!" Ropes tied to the opposite side of the moving lumber stack slowed and controlled the descent.

Using another timber on the ground, as a giant lever, raised one end of the lumber stack. "Roll them wheels right in here. Okay, you boys ease up gentle now, and we'll set this end down. Move over to the other end and put them wheels under that side!" Shorty instructed.

The labor-intensive move from the depot to Longhon Pine took five days before all the pieces of Elsie's new house finally occupied the dry grass overlooking Dust Creek. Jimmy's friends moved the heavy foundation timbers into place. Jimmy and Aaron spent all their time putting the house together. From time to time, when walls or timbers needed lifting, friends, neighbors and family threw parties at 'the Pine' and made a festive game of the labor.

Elsie's pregnant stomach gave her trouble walking up the extra steps to the front door of the finished house. Six months came and went since they had exchanged vows at the little church in San Benito. Aaron and Jimmy moved the modest bed up the stairs into the large bedroom of the unique house. Then the three sat on nail kegs at a table made from two barrels and an old shed door. Elsie and Jimmy owned no other furniture but Elsie was insistent, "I can't wait any longer. I'm moving in right now Jimmy, I don't care if there's no wash basin."

"Aaron, will you take Elsie over to Coalinga tomorrow morning and see if you can find a wash stand? I'm goin' to start digging a new trench for an outhouse a little closer."

Jimmy knew there was more involved in living outside town, but couldn't convince Elsie to stay in town until everything was finished. The next day, she gingerly worked her way down the steps of the house and picked up the water bucket. "I'm goin' down to the creek to fetch a pail of water." She said.

Jimmy, chin level with the ground, stood in his hole. "Now hold on a minute." He wore an expression of concern that amused Elsie. "I c'n do that. You shouldn't be luggin' water up the bluff!"

She grinned at him, "You look funny standing in your hole. You look all nervous and scared like the time you unbuttoned my blouse in the tall green grass." She held back her laugh. "I wasn't goin' to fill it all the way up," She giggled and ducked her head sideways, peering deeply into her lover's eyes.

Jimmy climbed out of his hole. "Maybe I can keep digging until I hit water, we can use it for a well then you won't have to lug water up from the creek."

Aaron rolled in early with Jimmy's parent's buckboard. "Boy, that hole is going pretty good." He said.

"Why don't you come along with us? That hole of yours will wait for you to come back." Elsie's eyes sparkled; she shrugged and tucked her chin in cheerful expectation. She knew he would say yes. He always said yes to her.

"Well, jump in. What're you waitin' for?" He teased her for laughing at his hole.

At the hardware store, silver haired Gunther Mintz,

who now owned two stores, asked the trio, “How’s dat house o’ yours comin’ Mrs. Longhon?” He treated all his friends and neighbors, with starched respect.

“It’s comin’ along just fine, Gunther. Jimmy’s been diggin’ a hole and I decided to move in. Last night was our first night there. Jimmy thinks we need some more kitchen furniture.”

“Well, yu know where dem new wash basins yu been watchin’ are.” Then Gunther turned to Jimmy, “What’s dat hole fer, young man?”

“It was goin’ to be for the out-house but I decided to keep on diggin’ ‘er down for a well.”

“Yu dun’t have tu be diggin’ that well now-a-days Mr. Longhon. We have dese here windmill pumps dat will du all de work fer yu, young man.”

He had seen the windmill at the depot a hundred times but hadn’t given it a thought. No windmills had been erected yet in San Benito except at the Freye place. “How do I get down to the water?”

“A feller comes out wit a steam drill and drills yu a hole and sinks a pipe right down tu de water!” Gunther deeply appreciated new technology and became excited talking about it.

Jimmy made arrangements for the well and ordered a windmill while Elsie and Aaron looked over furniture. The washbasin looked utilitarian, but the sofa, chest of drawers, and sideboard had beautiful lines and details. Elsie grinned and shrugged again when Jimmy walked up. She knew he would pretend to act hard and concerned then give in just to tease her. She loved him deeply and it showed in her sparkling, eager eyes.

"I really love the new sofa. Jimmy, you can take naps on it while I finish up supper in the afternoon." She continued to grin and chatter all the way back to Longhon Pine, the three of them bouncing along in the wagon full of precariously tied down furniture.

Chapter Twenty
-1892-

"Oh, this is so wonderful," she glowed, "Set the washstand and the side-board in the kitchen there right next to the stove."

Elsie couldn't have been happier. The boys set the new furniture in her kitchen right where she had envisioned.

Then the boys manhandled the chest of drawers up the tight staircase to the bedroom. Elsie already had all of Jimmy's well-worn dungarees neatly folded in wooden boxes along the wall. She finished filling the dresser from the boxes, then took the old boxes downstairs and stacked them as shelves in her new kitchen.

Jimmy finished his hole and built a closet sized shed around it, with a two-hole bench.

The windmill arrived in Coalinga a month after Jimmy placed the order.

Having ignored them too long, Jimmy rode out to check on his cattle. Aaron showed up at the house from San Benito after Jimmy had left. "Howdy, Elsie." Aaron said uncomfortably. "Is Jimmy gone out to the herd?"

Elsie picked up on his unusual behavior immediately. He squirmed from deep within looking shy and guilty; wearing the same expression other men had had on their faces when attempting advances that she had always repelled. She thought she would never have to deal with lonesome men ever again after her marriage to Jimmy. "Jimmy just went down toward the creek with Darlin'. Why don't you go on down there and find him?"

When Aaron left, she went into the house and dropped the inside latches so he couldn't get in without breaking something. She knew he was too shy to try anything like that. But, when Aaron came back to the house without Jimmy, as she knew he would, she didn't answer the door. She stayed in her room waiting for him to go away, and he finally did.

Elsie didn't say anything to Jimmy about Aaron's actions. Instead she gave the situation a lot of consideration. "Jimmy, I'm going to take the wagon into San Benito tomorrow and visit my mom."

"Want me to come along?" Jimmy asked expecting a sure come on ahead.

"If you have things to do, I'll be okay," She said, hoping he would let her go alone; and he did.

In San Benito, she found her mother bent over pulling weeds in the vegetable garden.

"You look like you're going to pop, Honey." Her mother greeted her.

"I feel like I'm going to, this belly of mine is too big." She replied then went on, "Ma, I've got to talk to you about somethin' and I don't want you to say anything to the neighbors." Elsie wanted to trust her mother to keep the story to herself but she was not sure. People in small towns had only one thing to do for diversion in those days, that was to gossip.

"You can trust me." Her mother assured her.

"Well, Aaron came pokin' around yesterday, acting all strange, well -- you know how men look at ya like they want somethin' but they don't know what it is. Anyway, I told him Jimmy was close by and to go find him. When he didn't find him he came back to the house and I wouldn't answer his knock."

"That was the right thing to do, Honey," her mother encouraged her.

"I love Aaron, and Jimmy loves him. He's done so much for us and asked so little, and I don't want anything to come between Jimmy and me. I can't come between Jimmy and Aaron. So I thought I'd drive over to the Hernandez place and invite them over for supper. Lina is a beautiful girl and spends all her time at their ranch. And I don't think she's got a boy calling on her. Why don't you and pa come out tomorrow and have supper too?" Elsie asked.

"That sounds good, Honey. I'll come with you tonight. Your father misses your cooking. He can come along tomorrow. I'll write your father a note so he'll know what's going on. You're right about Aaron, Elsie, and bringing Lisa in on it is a good idea," her mother said, as she scribbled a note to her husband then climbed up into the wagon next to Elsie.

Lina Saldoña, the oldest of the Saldoña girls, had wide shoulders and narrow hips. Long, straight, black hair that flowed down her back framed her rosy face and big, brown eyes.

"Hey Elsie, Mrs. Cutchel! ¿Que pasa?" She said excitedly, standing on the porch of the tidy adobe that had no door. "When is your baby due?"

"Any time." Elsie grinned placing an open hand high on her round side.

"How are you, Mrs. Cutchel? I haven't seen you for a long time! You look good." Lina exclaimed, happy to have guests.

"Where's your family?" Elsie wondered.

"They all went to help take a load of bricks out to the Freye's place this morning. They won't be home until late tomorrow." Lina explained.

"I came to invite you and the family out to our new house for supper." Elsie said.

"That would be wonderful," Lina exclaimed. "I never get to go anywhere. I don't think everybody else will be home early enough to make the trip."

"Will you come by yourself today, maybe stay the night?" Elsie asked.

"I have no way to get there or I would," said Lina

"How 'bout you come home with me?" Elsie tempted.

"Okay, I can feed the stock now, they might be a little hungry when the family gets home tomorrow but they'll be all right." Lina worried.

So the three ladies began portioning out dried ears of corn, and ground corn, and carrying it in wood and cloth buckets to all the penned farm animals near by the adobe.

Lina, Elsie and Mrs. Cutchel finally pulled the buckboard into the yard at Longhon Pine, Jimmy and Aaron were bent over assembling the windmill's blades.

"The drillers could be here any day and we better be sure this is ready to go," Jimmy said, knowing they were working out of curiosity more than necessity.

"Aaron, do you remember Lina?" Elsie asked.

"Sure I do, Elsie. Do you think I just fell off a turnip wagon?" He said softly attempting to be sarcastic.

Lina giggled at his response when Elsie stepped in, "Come on, Lina. Let's go inside and fix supper. We'll give you two a call when the food is ready."

Lina brought out Masa, cornflour she had ground in a stone metate earlier that day from hominy. This was the maize she made when she wanted to impress her friends. It had a special delicate and delicious flavor.

"Does Aaron have a girlfriend?" Lina asked Elsie as she flipped flat pieces of dough back and forth in her strong but soft hands.

"No, he doesn't, I'm pretty sure." Elsie said.

Feeling interest toward Aaron, Lina leaned out of the kitchen window, "Aaron, do you like corn tortillas?" she chirped up.

"I sure do." He said but she had already disappeared away from the window when he looked up.

"Bueno!" The empty window replied. "This is my secret maize recipe I grind from hominy."

"It's not a secret anymore." Aaron quipped back.

She grinned at her dough, with her mind outside as she continued patting the soft dough between her dainty fingers.

Elsie kept beans soaking in water everyday and rotated her clay pots, always having a portion soft and ready to cook. Mrs. Cutchel stewed some of Elsie's beans with a chicken Jimmy had killed and hung on the back porch earlier in the day.

"You boys ready por comida?" Lina called out to Jimmy and smiled brightly at Aaron.

"We're starving." Aaron replied.

"Pobrecito." She needled.

The five of them sat around the old shed door table on nail keg stools waiting for Elsie's father to arrive. The girls were doing most of the talking. That was okay with Aaron. He was a little shy around Lina.

"Oh!" Elsie bellowed "Oh!"

The pain in her belly and the water running down her legs told her all she needed to know. "The baby is coming, Jimmy! Oh! Take me upstairs. Oh!"

Aaron and Jimmy quickly took hold of Elsie's forearms, carefully hurrying her up the steep stairs. Mrs. Cutchel scurried up behind and Lina wiped up the trail of pink water.

"Maybe I should go into San Benito and fetch Elsie's father." Aaron suggested.

"He's on his way and should already be here." Elsie groaned.

I don't know if this is anything like calvin' or not!" Jimmy attempted to control his panic by talking more than usual.

"No, it's nada like calvin', you loco hombre!" Lina uttered.

"I don't like traveling after dark like this," Elsie's father worried. He traveled slowly and carefully along the dark uneven road. Had he known his daughter was in labor, he would have pushed along faster.

A half hour later, Jimmy's Mom, and Mr. Cutchel showed up at Longhon Pine at the same time.

Elsie couldn't sleep. Her contractions came often enough to keep her awake but too far apart to anticipate the birth. Elsie's mother and Dora Longhon stayed in with Lina and Elsie.

Lina went down to the kitchen, serving up beans, chicken and tortillas for everyone. The men were still not admitted into Elsie's room.

Elsie's father hung around downstairs with Jimmy and Aaron. With little else to do, the men sat and played poker around the old shed door table. Since none of them had any cash, they used corn seeds for currency to gamble with.

With nowhere for the boys to sleep, the rest of the night passed uncomfortably. The three of them took turns sleeping on the sofa. At sun up Jimmy lit the wood stove and heated the left over beans and chicken for breakfast. He brought portions for the girls upstairs in Elsie's room. With a firm hand Mrs. Cutchel continued to keep Jimmy at bay. "I'm okay Jimmy." Elsie wanted him to feel at ease.

After eating the boys were outside tinkering with the fan blades for the windmill. "Hey! Quiet down a second. Did you hear that?" Jimmy exclaimed then jumped to his feet, darted into the house and up the stairs three at a time to the doorway guarded by Jimmy's mother and Mrs. Cutchel. "You're a father, Jimmy, she's a little girl. Looks just like you. Elsie wants to name her Marcella Callidora Lina Longhon."

Everyone knew why -- Marcella because of Elsie's mother, Callidora because of Jimmy's mother Dora, then, of course, Lina for Lina. "Now you go back outside. We'll call you later for some lunch."

"But I have to see Elsie!" Jimmy complained.

"You can see her tonight." His mother said firmly but gently.

So the first of Jimmy and Elsie's daughters who became known through a complex series of nicknames as Marcalina, was born at Longhon Pine. Born when the house's unfinished condition could only supply enough furniture for the comfort of two people.

In the following fifteen years, Elsie and Jimmy had seven more girls.

The windmill lay close to Jimmy's outhouse for six more months waiting for the well drillers to show up. When they finally came and hit water, Elsie had walked up and down from the creek for so long that she didn't care if the well worked or not and it didn't. Somewhere in transport or lying in the yard for six months, the pump had gotten jammed. When Aaron, Lolo, Shorty and Jimmy finally raised the windmill tower to its feet and hooked up the shaft, nothing turned. The blades were stuck, bowing into the wind and back; making an *eek* sound, but not whirling and drooling water like the well at the depot in Coalinga.

Better at carpentry than mechanics, Jimmy built a wash-house for bathing and laundry close to the creek at the bottom of the trail that led down the bluff. A huge pot and stove for heating water kept the place warm and cozy.

And just about then, Mr. Mintz came around with an electric pump that pumped water all the way into the house. Over time the bathhouse by the creek turned into a place where the family enjoyed relaxing. It was also a fine place to have privacy when one felt overwhelmed.

-1913-

Life for the Longhons had gone on pleasantly for years like the illuminated pages out of a fairy tale book.

One Saturday evening, it was bath time for church the next day. Jimmy and his youngest daughter, three-year-old Elizabeth, sat together in the washtub in the laundry shed talking and splashing, when Elsie stepped in. She had a look of drawn agony that Jimmy had never seen on her face before.

"Lizzy. Jump out and run up to the house. Marci will help you find some clean clothes." Elsie paused in painful silence as the child dripped obediently past on tiptoes.

"Aaron dropped a telegram by." Elsie leaned against the door jam of the shed. Holding the telegram and cupping the elbow of her right arm in her left hand, she pinched her lower lip from side to side between her thumb and index finger.

She was solemn and distant. "It's from Los Angeles." She stated flatly. The pain in her chest and ribs were more intense than her worst struggles of childbirth. "It says your daughter Rosalita and her mother were taken hostage by Joaquin Murrieta."

Jimmy stood up in the washtub. His face so seriously sad, he frowned as deep a frown as ever seen on a man's face in San Benito. He knew Elsie now knew the most serious secret of his life in Los Angeles. He had never known how to tell Elsie, or anyone in San Benito for that matter. The gush of water down his body from the tub slowly reduced to a trickle. His muscular lanky shoulders hunched forward and down with the weight of the mental anguish he struggled under. His face, six days unshaven, tanned from the eyes down to his chest, showed a white forehead from the protection of his hat while out in the workday sun. His deep, sad eyes stared conflicted into Elsie's disappointed face. She stared back at the naked man she loved so dearly. The tops of his hands and halfway up his forearms radiated the same dark color as his cheeks. The skin surrounded by hair at the top of his legs appeared dark in contrast to his flat belly that glowed stoic white. She grimaced in pain, "How could you?" She choked on more tears, flinging the telegram at Jimmy, then turned and ran up the bluff.

Chapter Twenty-One

Jimmy didn't go to the house. He dressed in the clothes he had worn for the last six days. He smelled the contrast between his freshly bathed body and the pungent garments. Darlin' stood calmly while Jimmy picked clean the bottoms of her feet and saddled her. Then he rode toward Coalinga in a slow jog, the weight of his Buntline tugging at his side.

He rode past the depot in Coalinga, a very quiet place at seven o'clock in the far western evening -- to Whitey's place. "They figure Joaquin headed toward Fort Tajon on the Grapevine Trail then east toward Mojave. He's travelin' with five men," Whitey told Jimmy standing in front of his barn.

"When did they take the horses?" asked Jimmy.

"Five days ago," Whitey replied. "They're well on their way to Mojave by now. Harry Love and the California Rangers from Los Angeles are takin' it slow; they can't be riding into an ambush. I don't see what chance Joaquin thinks he might have of riding back into the valley without gettin' caught."

Jimmy detailed his thoughts as Whitey earnestly listened: "He must not think anybody north knows or cares about what he's done. He'll have to ride through Kings Canyon, or Yosemite, unless he plans on riding all the way north through Reno and across Lake Tahoe." He said. "We're far enough north that we could head 'em off if we made it straight 'cross the Sierra divide in time."

"What do you mean, we?" Whitey asked quietly. "Where's Aaron?"

Jimmy adjusted his eyes and fixed them sadly on Whitey. "He's stayin' back with Lina and watching over Longhon Pine."

"I'd come with you and show you how it's done if I weren't so dang old and tired." Whitey complained. "You could ride up the logging-camp roads behind Lake Isabella along the Kern river and through the Indian burial grounds and wait for them along the Mojave-Reno trail."

"Whitey, I think that's a fine idea but I can't do it without you. 'Sides you haven't left Coalinga in twenty years, have you?" Jimmy tried to bring a little levity from within his deep, serious mood.

"Ah hell, if I don't come along you'll probably git lost and be gone two more years. What would Elsie do then? She cain't up and marry Little Walt any more, he's such a gimp. Now there's somebody who ain't been off the ranch in ten years."

Finally packed and underway, the two men, on horseback, angled across the grassy plain of central California toward the Sierra foothills, the Kern River, and Lake Isabella. The ride to Lake Isabella consumed seven days. They only covered twenty to twenty-five miles a day but the felons could ride no faster than Jimmy and his posse of one.

"When we hit the Kern, we follow her east into the

foothills. We'll have to cross her twice, just before the lake and then a ways beyond." Whitey instructed.

"The river's low this time o' year so it won't be no bother to cross her anywhere we feel like." Jimmy added.

Ten days passed. The men wound up through the rolling grassy foothills, and squinted their eyes against the bright, white boulders that lined the river's banks. The final twenty miles, before the Indian meadows, were steep and monotonous. Curving away and out of sight of the river, the trail switched back every quarter mile. The horses huffed and puffed, grunting their deep urge to turn back with every breath.

At the divide, the trail leveled off, passing through marvelous stands of pines for many miles, then descended across and onto the Eastern Sierra. The long meadows of shaggy, green grass followed the course of the Kern, which was not much more than a wide creek at that elevation. Few had seen that amazing scene, probably because fourteen miles east the trail wandered dangerously close to the treacherously steep face of granite walls that looked out over the high desert below the Eastern Sierra. With such a difficult route, any traveler would either need a good reason to attempt crossing the mountains at the meadows, or have to be absolutely lost.

"Let's camp right there tonight." Whitey pointed at the spot where the trail crossed the river.

"I think I'd rather hunker down 'bove the river in

them rocks so we can hide a little camp fire and watch out over the trail for anyone coming along." Jimmy motioned Whitey's attention to the huge, smooth granite boulders rising out of the grass about three hundred yards off the trail.

"I s'pose you might have a point there," Whitey agreed. "For a greenhorn," He added.

The horses needed food and time to recoup their energy from the long climb, giving Jimmy and Whitey a good reason to rest their backsides.

Whitey, an early riser, watched the sky turn from black to gray to blue in the chilly hours of the morning. Whitey also watched a small campfire, two miles along the trail, wafting a straight line of white smoke very high into the windless air.

"Jimmy!" Whitey whispered gruffly. "I'm goin' t' check on the camp up ahead on the trail. Maybe they'll 'vite me f'r breakf'st."

"Okay." Jimmy turned in his sleep. "I'll be 'long."

Whitey saddled up, climbed the side of his horse, and headed northeast, high and wide around the canyon wall, well above the trail, giving him a long, clear view of the camp below. Two horses stood munching grass. There was, however, no sign of an entire herd. Nine figures moved about calmly. Two squaws, two braves and five children worked in preparation for the day.

Jimmy followed along in the footprints left by

Whitey's horse. Jimmy was three-hundred yards behind. Whitey squeezed his legs together, urging his horse to walk out from the pines where they had been standing and watching the activity below. The horses in the Indian camp pricked their ears in his direction and let out a long call. Whitey's horse responded. The small band of Mojave Indians setting up their summer camp watched suspiciously at the stranger riding toward them.

Whitey stopped fifty yards from the camp, straightened his knees, pressed his feet into the stirrups and stood in the saddle. He held both of his upper arms level with his shoulders his forearms bent at the elbows, palms toward the squatters, as proof he held no weapon and intended a friendly visit. "How." He said earnestly.

The eldest brave stood erect and attentive, staring at Whitey for a very long time. "How." He returned.

The elder allowed his eyes to scan the surrounding trails, hills, and brush. He then tilted his head back with an inquisitive gesture toward Jimmy, who sat astride Darlin' under the same growth of pines where Whitey had been sitting for so long watching the native's camp.

"Esta es mi amigo y esta su amigo." With inadequate hand signs Whitey tried to explain that Jimmy was his friend and traveling companion.

Reluctantly, the elder waved Whitey in and presumed Jimmy would follow. The five children stood shyly close together, staring up at the unusual looking visitors, saying nothing, attentive to their every move.

Cautiously, the brave stepped forward. With more laughable attempts between them, the result of the conversation brought coffee and a small tin pot out of Whitey's saddlebags. This made the little band of natives very happy. A portly woman poured water out of a tar-lined basket into Whitey's pot. The six adults, including Jimmy and Whitey, squatted around the fire waiting for the water to boil. Whitey's desire for his early morning Arbuckle turned into an inadvertent peace offering and broke the ice.

The amusing communication between everyone on hand, including the children, became quite enjoyable. A peculiar combination of Mojave, English, Spanish, and sign language ensued. The children were laughing so hard they were rolling on the ground. A great deal of news changed hands between the strangers with the humorous translations.

The most interesting bit of information for Jimmy was related to the story about a herd of horses trailed by five men and a young lady heading from the east in their direction up the treacherous trail from the desert below.

"Well, there y'are, Scourge." Whitey teased Jimmy, "They're comin' to you after all." Whitey needlessly clarified, his excitement growing.

"I guess we ought to kick outa here and see what's what." Jimmy replied

He awkwardly signed some thank-yous and cordial comments with his hands. Then tightened the cinch on Darlin's saddle, stepped up, and left Whitey still sipping coffee with the cheerful tribe.

The pines thinned and the crags above stood out more ominously as Jimmy rode east. Then, without forewarning, the trail narrowed and curved sharply north to the left. To the southeast, the land fell away steeply, dangerously, all but vertical, three hundred yards down. The view out over the desert amazed Jimmy. And there on the same trail, halfway down the steep face, rode the Comancheros. At that distance, Joaquin Murrieta, the devil incarnate, could not be seen.

From photos Jimmy new to watch for a man with hair, parted in the middle, cut equal length around a flat round head level with his chin, tied at his forehead with a rolled, grayed blue, paisley, scarf. Everyone who met him remembered his tiny eyes and fat wide chin. When he spoke it was a muffled bark of quiet orders. Rosalita as well as his posse were intensely frightened of the loathsome villin.

The long line of their trail dust brightly backlit by the morning sun, drifted above the desert, marking their movement up the mountain.

Jimmy rode slowly to keep his trail dust from telling Joaquin of his presence on the mountain. The cliff fell away steeply on his right as he crept down hill. He watched attentively up the hill on the left for a place to hide Darlin' and wait. Then it appeared, a wide flat dead-end opening to the northwest uphill side of the narrow trail. A camouflaged opening on

Jimmy's left, a leafy manzanita draw perfect for him to hide Darlin', wait for the marauders and make his ambush. He rode into the thick brush. He followed a deer trail around behind a huge bolder on his right. There he tied Darlin' to some manzanita, and belly-crawled to the top of the boulder. He lay down to wait. The trail was very narrow and only allowed one rider to travel at a time.

Jimmy watched cautiously as the lead rider passed so close he could smell the horse. He was followed closely by a long string of horses in single file. Then another rider came along in line. Jimmy heard him softly mutter in a deep guttural tone, "This dust is goin' to choke me to death."

Four men passed in the same manner. Then, Jimmy saw Rosalita and mistook her for Rosa. She was bent in her saddle, miserably following the horse in front of her. Jimmy pointed his Buntline past her and carefully took aim at the last rider in the column. Gently he squeezed the trigger and blew the man out of his saddle, sending him crashing over the steep edge of the trail into the cactus and rocks below.

Instantly, in response to his shot, the echo of more guns reverberated off the flat walls on the opposite side of the canyon. Chaos exploded on the trail. Horses were forced from the edge to their death in the dusty struggle.

Rosalita's horse lunged frantically about in the melee. It uselessly staggered in the turmoil, mindlessly refusing to go forward as Rosalita spurred him on. The narrow trail afforded little room to turn around, and then her crazy horse stepped backwards hysterically toward the edge of the trail and the steep cliff below. Its right hind hoof barely caught enough ground to support its weight, and it teetered backwards on top of the cliff.

When the horse reached out it felt nothing under its other hind leg and overextended it searching in thin air for some ground to push off from.

All of the horses scrambling, threw Rosalita's horse further off balance. Jimmy watched the dreadful sight with clenched teeth. Her horse reared backward on one hoof at the edge of oblivion. Wildly distressed, the beast lunged off its right hind leg throwing rocks and gravel into the air away from the cliff. Then he pounded across the narrow trail, through the brush where Jimmy waited dumbfounded, on Darlin'. As Rosalita came close, her horse running past, Jimmy reached out and hooked her around the waist, pulling her off her horse and onto Darlin' with him.

"Rosa! Where's Rosalita?" Jimmy shouted.

"What! Where's Rosalita? I'm Rosalita. Who are you?" She screamed in a panic.

With no time to waste, Jimmy pressed Darlin' into the draw, through the brush, farther up from the main trail.

A little farther from the chaos and the gunfire, he rephrased his question. Rosalita began to cry. She couldn't control her eyes or lips or tightly wrinkled forehead. "My mother's dead." She gulped. It took great effort to force out the words. She cried with a chugging grunting sound impossible to describe, it wavered despondently at the end.

"I know. I know. Try not to cry and tell me what happened?" Jimmy asked anxiously. There was solace for her in crying. But Jimmy was feeling intolerant of his daughter whom he just met.

"Below, on the desert," She repeated her throaty, gulping crying sound, again and again. Slowly, she forced out the words, "Last night we turned west into the foothills along this trail. Just below the steep grade we made camp. My mother quietly stood next to Joaquin, holding the horse they made her ride. Without saying anything, she pulled the gun from his holster and shot him. Without blinking, all the bandits drew and fired their guns into her at the same time. She died I think before she laid herself down on the loose, coarse sand. The bullet she fired went through high on Joaquin's belly. He couldn't talk. He seemed dead except he lay there all night, shivering, barely breathing, and staring at the sky. Sometime in the night, he died. By the morning, he was stiff."

"I'm very sorry." Jimmy consoled his daughter he hadn't seen since she was an infant. The stunning, disheveled, young women in his arms resembled Rosa in every detail. "I'm your father," he confessed sadly.

"You're not!" She said, but she knew deep within that he told the truth. "My father deserted my mother and me! My mother hated you!" she slipped. "My mother hated you for leaving, and will never forgive you! Not even from her grave!"

There was nothing Jimmy could have said to the bright vivid doppelgänger of the woman he met along the cienegas in the Old Pueblo de Los Angeles.

In the gun battle along the trail, Whitey and the two Mojave braves ambushed and killed all the horse thieves. Then the five survivors carefully drove the herd back down the narrow trail to a spot marked by vultures and crows. The birds, hopped, circled and danced in the wind and sand. Jauquin, stripped of his belongings, wore only pants and his shirt, soaked with blood. His eyes were gone, pecked out by the scavenger birds.

A crow stood on a rock fifty feet away, holding a string in its beak. The index finger from Joaquin's left hand dangled at the end of the string. The disgusting Joaquin had kept his finger as a trophy on the string around his neck. He lost it in a knife fight many years ago.

The two Mojave braves went up to Joaquin's body and began to chant to be sure the vile man didn't somehow come back to life.

Jimmy and Rosalita couldn't look at Rosa. Whitey straightened out her dress and hair as best he could, but she too had lost her eyes to the vultures and crows. Working in the hot sun, Whitey dug as deep a hole as he could and gently laid the woman in it. Rosalita and Jimmy helped gather stones to lie on top of Rosa's grave. Neither Jimmy nor Rosalita prayed out loud. They stood quietly, listening to the Mojave death chants and remembered Rosa in the silence of their souls.

"These horses belong to Juanita Vermond, the Woman with Many Horses." Jimmy said, gesturing toward the herd. He had recognized the brand earlier on the trail. "I guess we'd better trail 'em back to the Pueblo 'n bring Rosalita home."

She stared at Jimmy with disgust. Again she choked and struggled not to cry, but did, this time longer and sadder with unbearable pain in her face and chest. She stared at Jimmy, her head tilted with admonition, her mouth slightly open filled with phlegm and more pouring from her nose. "Home?" She could barely breathe. "Where's that? Where do you think I have a home?" She demanded. "Back in Los Angeles I will be expected to be a whore. Do you know what a WHORE is? --- FATHER! Every man knows Joaquin took me. Everyone in Los Angeles knows what he did to me on the trail." She again tried not to, but sobbed. She felt she had no one and honestly and urgently wished for her life to end.

Jimmy stood shocked and silent. Tactlessly conflicted about Rosa and Elsie, he had absolutely no solution for the situation.

"Well then, gal, you'll come to Longhon Pine and live there with your father." Whitey stated.

Something about the influence of Whitey's voice,

something in Jimmy's memories of this lifelong authority figure, told him no matter what the consequences, he couldn't argue.

"You'll come and live with me, Rosa." Jimmy said quietly.

She looked up, wondering through her tears, *Was it a slip of his tongue or was she no longer little Rosa?*

"I don't think there is a place for me there." She rejected his offer. "I don't know you! My mother's gone!" She was dying inside, but the thought of her father there to take care of her helped a tiny bit.

The braves walked up to Jimmy and handed him a burlap sack heavy with the weight of what seemed like a stone but oozed blood. Then they wandered back up the steep trail that led to the meadows. The bag contained the hand and head of the detestable Joaquin Murrieta. Jimmy tied it to the back of his saddle; then he, Whitey, and Rosalita pushed the ramuda along the trail toward Los Angeles.

At the eastern trail head where it made a "T" with the Reno-Mojave trail, they found the California State Rangers who were really just a bunch of overpaid cowardly thugs, who were camped, drunk and arguing over whether to go on or head back to Los Angeles. "We'll never git 'round them fellers on the meadows trail. All that shootin' we been hearing means more trouble; they prob'ly just killed a whole clan of Mojave's. They'll see us comin' from above, ambush us, and kill every one of us f'r sure."

“They won’t be killin’ anymore,” Whitey broke in, and startled the group. “Jimmy here’s got the devil’s head and hand tied to his saddle.”

Not wanting anymore to do with the disgusting thing, he untied it and tossed it to the constable. “Here, Harry, you c’n say you got ‘im.” And the constable did just that. Everyone in the state of California thinks that Captain Harry Love shot and killed Joaquin Murrieta, when all along it was Rosa Ramirez.

Chapter Twenty-Two

Jimmy's unlikely group of not quite Vaqueros pushed the herd of horses right through downtown Los Angeles, past Jimmy's hotel, past the adobe where Jimmy shot Victor, past the cienegas, across the shallow river, and out to the woman with many horses' -- Juanita Vermund's ranch.

She stood up on her porch when she heard the horses coming.

"Loose somethin', Vermund?" Jimmy asked glad to see his old friend.

"Well, I never thought I'd lay eyes on you again this side of hell," She sang out. "By the sound of their dainty feet running up here in front of you I'd say you must have lost eight of my fine horses out gallivanting around in the dust."

With his hat off his head, held respectfully against his chest, Whitey ceremoniously orated, "We all thought the same thing in Coalinga seventeen years ago, but he showed up back on our doorstep unexpectedly the same as he has here at yours. Howdy, Miss Vermund. I'm Whitey Whitmore, Railroad agent and wilderness guide to Jimmy Longhon, the Scourge of the West. And by the way, your count was dead on. We lost exactly eight head of your splendid steeds out there on the villainous dusty trail"

"Well! I think I've heard about you." She exclaimed. "Wilderness guide! I am impressed."

Rosalita and Jimmy felt the electricity between the two senior citizens. Juanita's appearance was an interesting combination of youth and age. Her deep wrinkles and long gray hair opposed her slim, muscular body. She hopped into the saddle and had all the horses penned up in short order, with a little help from her guests.

"Rosa, let's you 'n me leave these two love birds alone 'n go see the hotel and Alonzo." Jimmy said to his daughter.

Alonzo hadn't changed in the seventeen years since Jimmy left Rosa and Los Angeles in 1890. His hair hadn't grayed and his skin contained the same taut smoothness except for some slight crow's feet wrinkles in the corners of his eyes.

"I'm sorry about your mother," Alonzo said to Rosalita, when his two friends that he knew so well walked into his office. "I loved her very much."

"Gracias." Rosalita whimpered and collapsed into his

arms. During the years Rosalita was growing up, Alonzo took the part of papa because of Jimmy's absence.

"You've finally returned, amigo. Tell me how your life has gone all these years." Alonzo inquired.

"Well 'lonzo, ain't much t' say, really. I married Elsie and she gave me seven beautiful daughters. I run 'bout a thousand head of range cattle on the open graze 'tween Dust Crick and Coalinga, which keeps me busy, dawn 'til dusk, six and a half days a week. What about you, Alonzo? What's been keeping you going all these years?"

"Running your hotel and restaurant. You've been my best customer and I haven't seen nor talked to you in all this time. You have done well here, Jaime, better than most," Alonzo explained. "What are your plans, now? Has anything changed?"

"Rosalita will come to San Benito with me. I haven't talked to Elsie since your telegram arrived. She couldn't have been more sad or angry when she read the message. But I'll go back 'n try patchin' things up. Seems we've been together too long to let this permanently ruin the family."

"I hope you are right, amigo. What shall I do with your holdings here? Do you know you have over five-hundred-thousand dollars in the bank? I've been paying myself ten percent of the gross every year. Giving Rosa an allowance for herself and Rosalita. Reinvesting ten percent of the gross and saving the profits to turn over to Rosalita if you failed to someday return. Now that you are back, what should I do?"

"Mind running it like ya been?" Jimmy asked. "I'm not that good with hotels and cafes. Maybe you could invest ten percent of the capitol into somethin' new and modern like those electric lights or telephones or somethin."

Alonzo perked up, "I've been reading about a fellow named Henry Ford, who intends to start building thousands of gasoline-powered automobiles. He claims he will replace horses and carriages in twenty years. One of his representatives arrived today. He's going to give a demonstration tomorrow at the depot."

"Well, let's stop over and have us a look. What d'ya say, Alonzo?"

"Si, amigo. I'll meet you here at nine. Okay? Then, hasta mañana, Jaime."

"Adios, Tio." Rosalita waved as she and Jimmy left the office to check into the Hotel de Los Angeles.

In the morning, a crowd gathered around the four Model-T automobiles lined up carefully in the big vacant lot in front of the depot. The automobiles had shiny, black paint and black leather tops. Two had the tops up and two were folded down neatly around the back seat.

A striking young man dressed in a very handsome suit

of clothes stood up on the raised walk around The Pueblo de Los Angeles depot and said. “Ladies and Gentlemen! Boys and Girls! Allow me to direct your attention down the road to your left! *That*, my friends, is the future of America!”

Puttering up the road from the south of the spectators, winding along the course of the river, trundled an odd sight, a carriage without horses. More modern-looking than a carriage, however, the automobile reminded Jimmy of the day he first saw the train on the trip to visit his Aunt in Stockton when he was twelve years old. This thing looked equally impressive and powerful in its modern style,yet so compact. The Model-T rumbled up, popped a few puffs of smoke and squealed to a halt, to everyone’s delight.

“Este es muy estupendo? Rosalita absent-mindedly asked her newfound father.

“Yes, ‘tis.” He answered continuing to stare at the vehicles without looking at his daughter. “I’d like to take that thing for a lope around town.” Jimmy said to the salesman.

“Well, sir,” The salesman explained, “This is a very complex device and requires excellence in timing, coordination, and judgment. However,” he said eyeing the lean cowboy with the unusual guns, “I’m sure you can learn.”

“Come on, honey.” Jimmy pressed his hand against Rosalita’s back and stepped up to the vehicle. “Show me what to do, mister. Maybe I'll buy my daughter one of these before we head home."

"Where's home, my good man?" The salesman asked.

"A few miles outside of Coalinga on Dust Creek." Jimmy answered.

"Well, that's fine, because you'll need to be close to the railroad to ship in gasoline. Now, then, let me explain the operation of the Ford Model-T automobile. This is your throttle: it increases or decreases the speed at which the engine turns by allowing more or less fuel to run into the combustion chambers ..."

After fifteen minutes of directions, Jimmy and Rosalita climbed in. The salesman walked around to the front and yelled, "Contact!" Jimmy flicked the switch nervously, his hands wet with sweat. The salesman grabbed the crank and leaned into it, giving the engine three good twirls whereupon the machine stammered to life while the salesman pulled the crank away and jumped for his life. Jimmy let the clutch peddle out too fast and the engine grabbed hold. Both Rosalita's and her father's heads were flung back as the auto lunged forward clipping the salesman's thigh as he jumped. Jimmy turned hard to the left to avoid running down the crowd. The momentum came close to throwing Rosalita out of the vehicle. At the same time his hat, caught by the wind, blew off into the street.

"Areeeeba!" Rosalita screamed at the top of her lungs, all the time laughing uncontrollably. They raced around wildly, churning up dust and gleefully howling with pleasure.

Then the two lurched to a stop at the crowd. "How much money do you want for this?" Jimmy demanded.

"They're two hundred and ninety dollars, sir. How many would you like?" The salesman pressed eagerly.

"We'll take two, mister! Alonzo, you better have a ride in this. I never laughed so hard in my life!" Jimmy encouraged his friend.

"Jimmy, I think this might be the perfect investment. Let's make a deal with him to buy all his stock and distribute the machines here in Los Angeles!" Alonzo anxiously suggested.

"That'll do fine, Alonzo. You make the proposition. Use whatever it takes and set us up in business. We'll be fifty-fifty partners. Call it Longo Automobiles. I trust ya to make the right decisions." Jimmy told his old business manager.

Rising before sunup the next day, Jimmy and Rosalita began their dusty, bumpy trip north, at first light. Before they left, Jimmy arranged to have Darlin', the second Model-T, and four hundred gallons of gasoline shipped by train to Coalinga. They carried along sixty extra gallons of the fuel in four fifteen-gallon cans tied to the rear bumper. At thirty miles per hour they arrived in Coalinga around twelve o'clock noon and passed through under the shocked scrutiny of two young boys walking along the road.

Hee-ah! Hee-ah! Jimmy honked the horn as they passed.

The sun was still above the horizon when the two automobilists drove into the homestead at Longhon Pine. "This 's it, Honey! But nobody seems to be around. I bet she uprooted all those girls and has 'em sleepin' on the floor and barn at her ma's house in San Benito."

"What are we going to do?" Rosalita asked.

Jimmy had unbuckled his gun belt, climbed up on a chair, reached over his head, gun-belt in hand, and buckled it around the open beam in the kitchen. From up on the chair he looked down and said, "I ain't sure. I suppose we should fetch us somethin' to eat and get a good night's rest and figure out the rest in the mornin'."

They went to work together in the kitchen and talked.

"I don't want to cause any trouble with your real family." Rosalita sighed, still not sure what to call Jimmy.

"Real family? Rosa, you're my daughter, and I love you, and that's as real as it gits. Life is a twisty, turny deal of the cards that nobody can plan. No matter how hard anyone tries, somethin'll come up every inch of the way 'n change all the plans. Why, look at you. You're the spittin' image of your mother. I wouldn't of knowed the difference. Now, here you are right in the middle of my life and I wouldn't want it any different." Jimmy explained earnestly. "So that's just the way it's going to be from now on."

"What about your wife? She might want it different," Rosalita said then turned her attention to the squeak of the kitchen door, and the appearance of seven wet-haired, freshly bathed young ladies and their mother.

"Want what different?" Elsie asked, stiffly. She knew the beautiful young woman sitting at her table must be Jimmy's daughter. Elsie acted jealous so her husband would know how mad she was. She still cared but wasn't going to let Jimmy know, even though she was sure he knew more than he would say.

"Well, Elsie. I didn't know you were here." Jimmy said surprised. "This here's Rosalita."

Rosalita felt ashamed and embarrassed and didn't know what to say. "Hi," was her only timid response as she peeked up from looking down at her hands.

Jimmy and Elsie's little daughters stood in the kitchen huddled together watching the nervous look on their father's face.

"What's she doin' here?" Lizzy chirped up, enchanted by the strange lady in her home so late at night.

"You shush for now Lizzy. I'm sorry Rosalita. I'm Elsie, your father's wife. I want you to feel at home. Go up stairs with the girls. We'll talk about all this in the morning."

"But Ma!" Lizzy insisted.

"She's your sister you've never met. Take her

upstairs and show her your room. She'll sleep with you tonight," instructed Elsie.

The little girls were very excited to have a new sister so beautiful as Rosalita. They took her by the hand and wouldn't stop talking. Rosalita quietly towered above the covey of excited little ladies. They escorted her with delight up to their room.

Besides her age and height, Rosalita's appearance, brown skin, brown eyes, long black hair was very different from Jimmy's little blue eyed, light complected children. "How can you be our sister if we've never seen you before?" Little Lizzy asked, sincerely, oblivious of her physical differences.

"That's a long story. Come on, I'll tell you." Rosalita said kindly to her new sisters. For the first time in her life the emotional feelings of family ties began to permeate her heart and soul.

"I wanna brush your hair when you tell us!" Lizzy insisted, only willing to take yes for an answer.

The girls helped Rosalita get cleaned up for bed. Lizzy brushed and braided Rosalita's hair. "Your hair is so thick and smooth," Lizzy couldn't stop stroking the marvelous locks.

"That really feels good, Lizzy."

The fascinating thing about it, Rosalita wasn't Jimmy's daughter at all. The little girl was Alonzo's misbegotten heir. But, everybody that knew Jimmy or Rosa, or had anything to do with the Hotel de Los Angeles, assumed the child was Jimmy's. On the face it appeared Rosa was Jimmy's love.

Only Juanita Vermond truly knew the truth about Alonzo and Rosa. One morning before Jimmy moved his herd north, on her way into town, Juanita rode passed Jimmy heading out to work his cattle. She walked in unwittingly on Alonzo and Rosa when she stopped in to see him about suspicious horse records. After Jimmy's complaining, Juanita firmly knew Alonzo was the only possible explanation for Rosa's little girl.

Elsie stared at Jimmy sternly. "How can she be their sister if they've never seen her before?" Elsie asked sarcastically. "Why didn't you tell me about this, Jimmy? Do you know how I feel?"

"Seems you're pretty mad, but not so mad that you're gone, and that's what I 'spected." Jimmy replied humbly. But he didn't know the truth about Rosalita. Had he known, it wouldn't have mattered to him. As in the past he would have taken care of circumstances for the best interest of everyone concerned.

"Well, you 'spected wrong! I'm still here, and the girls are still here! Aaron and Lina and their younguns are still here, and we've been workin' the calves while you've been off scourgin' the west with Whitey! And I'm damn mad, and if I'da known 'bout your devilish ways when you came traipsin' back seventeen years ago I'd never of married you! But since you was so good at keepin' it a secret for all those years, and since you worked so hard and made such a damn good father for all those years, I'm goin' to give you a second chance! But no more kids or women better come showin' up at our doorstep or I'm goin' to take Little Walt's long gun down from over the door and shoot you!" She said seriously almost hysterically.

Jimmy sat staring at his hands, absorbing everything that Elsie hollered. He loved her so dearly and clearly understood the pain she was enduring. He'd never heard her use any profanity in all the years he'd known her, and knew her monologue came truthfully from her heart. "There ain't no more women or youngi ..."

"I won't hear it! You git down to the creek and fetch Rosalita a pail of water to wash up with. I'll go up and check on the girls." Elsie decreed.

Covered by a cloudy sky, Longhon Pine hadn't seen the sun since Jimmy and Rosalita rode up in the Model-T. Day after day a light mist fell from the sky early in the mornings but ceased toward noon. The sky remained overcast and gradually darkened ominously as the days passed after their arrival home.

Feeling guilty and not wanting to test the waters, Jimmy slept in the barn for three days while the wind outside became warm and humid. He spent more hours than normal catching up on his work around the ranch. Elsie's melancholy mood intensified under the overcast skies.

Then, on the fourth night after Jimmy's return, a light steady rain began at supper. Long after the girls had gone to sleep, the rain fell progressively harder. Elsie couldn't stand the solitude any longer. She tiptoed in her cotton flannel nightgown through the house and slipped out the back door. Her nightclothes clung to her skin from the soaking rain. By fair means or foul, Jimmy knew she was coming since he wasn't asleep, and heard her familiar footsteps crossing the wet yard. Lying in the hay, facing toward the barn doors, he opened his eyes. He didn't shift his body. He heard the rusty hinges as Elsie opened the huge doors. His heart pounded with curious uncertainty, like the day he opened her blouse in the tall green grass so long ago. She walked to the hay-pile where his blankets were spread. She pulled the wet nightgown off over her head, squatted down, lifted the blankets, and slid up against Jimmy's warm back. "Hi," She whispered. "I can't sleep."

The two partners lay awake late into the night, talking, loving and happy to have each other's friendship back. The rain pattered steadily on the barn roof but caused no concern to the occupants.

Elsie came to love Rosalita as her own daughter. Rosalita's focus, hard work, sense of humor, and love of her new family, surpassed her beauty. She never married and never knew a man after her arrival at Longhon Pine. She applied her motherly instincts to her little sisters and then on to her nieces and nephews. The pain and fear from her ordeal with Joaquin quietly tortured her all the rest of her life. And because she never complained or shared her pain no one knew but her. The girls came to love her in return and accepted her without hesitation.

Epilogue

The years swept by in a blink of an eye. The girls grew into women. Marci, the first to marry, and her husband, built a house along the lane that ran from the San Benito/Coalinga Road to the Longhon Pine homestead. Grandchildren and great-grandchildren and great great grandchildren came along. It seemed every generation of kids at Longhon Pine had a counter part in grand-foals from Darlin's lineage. Darlin' had passed on shortly after the last trip to Los Angeles in 1913.

Elsie passed on in 1953 at the age of eighty. Jimmy turned lonely and cranky but felt he needed to run the Smokin'-T outfit and be sure it made enough money to support the family. His granddaughter, Rosy, lived with him in the original store-bought Victorian with her husband and three girls. Jimmy didn't have a problem with that. After all the years of raising his girls, it felt natural to live with a house full of little ladies. At Elsie's funeral, he loosened the locket shaped like hands in prayer from around Elsie's still neck and took it away with him. From then on, he kept it in his left pant pocket and rubbed it between his thumb and middle finger.

It seemed Jimmy would live forever by the time his hundred and seventh birthday rolled around. At that point he never went far. He just sat in his rocker overlooking Dust Creek and out over the wild barley. A scene that he hadn't seen change in nearly a hundred years, and at least since the day he had proposed to Elsie.

The windmill he ordered and set up never did work. Electricity finally brought water right into the house. Nobody knew what to do with the old windmill so it just stood there as a souvenir irritating Jimmy. "Damn old thing, anyway!" He would gripe, sitting in his rocker.

Without warning, on the twenty-second of April 1983, the land at Longhon Pine began to roll and heave. It reminded Jimmy of the motion of a wild bucking horse, but the size of a mountain. Jimmy and his rocker were both tossed off the porch and thrown six feet into the yard. The rocker landed upright, at first seemingly okay, then immediately flopped over on its side. Jimmy hadn't lost his seat in the rocker and remained upon the ground on his side for a few seconds, hoping he had died. Realizing he hadn't, he struggled to his feet. He straightened up the rocker, bent forward and walked toward the bluff. Again the ground rolled beneath him, and he crouched with his arms out to balance himself but plopped onto his bottom. The roof above the porch where he had been sitting a moment before collapsed and crashed onto the wooden deck.

A sight he hadn't seen in seventy years then appeared on the distant horizon. The clouds that looked like horsemen in the sky charged from the heavens directly over his head. He turned as they passed over the windmill and into eternity on the opposite side of the sky. Then all fell silent. The sun glared on the dry, dusty ground. Out of nowhere the still air began to stir.

The windmill's tail creaked and turned the blades into the wind and then they caught the breeze. Without apparent reason the blades began to turn and the windmill came to life. "Damn that thing anyway." He complained, "Now I don't need it and it starts pumpin'."

Rosy, Jimmy's fifty-year-old granddaughter, ran around the house from the back, saw the crushed porch, and screamed.

"I'm all right," He complained again.

She looked across the yard to the bluff where Jimmy stood staring past the windmill, shouting at the sky. The old weathered chair rocked back and forth on its own in the yard. "Damn you, Russ! Damn you, Pots! Damn you, Cisco! I want t'go with you! Wait for me!"

That's when another most unexpected thing came about. An old codger who Jimmy didn't recognize at first rolled into the yard in a rusty old Dodge pick-up truck and pulled up next to Jimmy. The driver wore a dirty old white-felt cowboy hat. The whites of his eyes were very cloudy. The end of his nose had chunks of unruly skin growing from it, as did his ear lobes, hanging almost to his shoulders. He didn't have a light in his eyes. He stared at Jimmy stiffly and began to talk in a monotone growly whisper. "You still talkin' to the clouds, Long Gun? You haven't changed a bit. I came by to say I'm sorry for takin' shots at you, all those times. And thanks for helpin' me out when my horse trashed me that time. That horse 's been dead now for 'bout eighty years." Walt laughed to himself a little in his crotchety old voice. "I heard you had a daughter down there in the Pueblo."

Slowly recognizing the man's cut away lip Jimmy felt a surge of faint recollection. "You're Little Walt, ain't ya!" He said. "I ain't seen your ugly old mug since the last time you tried to kill me. That's been about a hundred years, ain't it?"

"Well, I reckon. I've been more 'an little embarrassed about all the trouble I caused out here. Thought I'd wait a while 'fore I came a-callin'. You still mad at me?" Walt inquired directly.

"Ah, hell, no! To tell the truth, I figured you'd died 'n didn't tell no one." Jimmy joked with a serious look on his wrinkled old face.

"Nah, I ain't dead yet. Should be, but I guess the Good Lord is givin' me a little more time up here 'fore he sends me to hell," Little Walt grumbled.

"Serves you right. I wish he'd take me so's I c'n catch up with ol' Russ 'n Elsie. I miss 'em terrible." A light twinkled in Jimmy's eyes. "Hey now, I j'st 'membered sompn' -- come on in the house here." The two old codgers walked very slowly toward the house and struggled up the steps. Little Walt, still walked all bent over because of the trashing his horse gave him under the oak tree so many years ago. They carefully negotiated their way over the fallen porch roof and to the front door. "I reckon I've got somethin' here, belongs to you." Jimmy climbed up on a wooden chair and precariously reached the rafter were he hung the old German gun eighty-five years before. "I always said I wouldn't give it back to ya 'til ya come 'n apologized, and here you are, so there ya go. It's that fancy shootin' long gun ya used to tote around with ya a long time ago."

"Well all be!" Little Walt gasped, seriously straight-faced staring at the gun. "I wondered what happened to that old thing."

- That's It For Now Folks -

Glossary

Adobe Brick – *Building block made of clay and sand mixed with water and straw*
Andale – *Do it fast*
Arbuckle's – *Cup of Coffee*
Bandito – *Robber, thief, murderer*
Buckaroo – *Cowboy good at riding wild horses*
Buckboard – *Four wheeled horse drawn wagon*
Buntline - *Long-barreled colt single action army revolver*
Cattle – *Bovine, herding animals, plural*
Cienegas – *Marshes*
Circadian - *Recurring naturally on a twenty-four-hour cycle*
Coaling Station – *Steam train station for fuel and water*
Come a ti yi yippy yippy yea - *Around cattle, kai yea` was a Sioux Indian word meaning move it or get moving – Just a fun thing to say when playing cowboy*
Compadres – *Literally, "co-father" or "co-parent" relationship between the parents and godparents of a child aka close friends*
Compañeros - *Companions*
Cow pony – *Horse trained to herd cattle*
Conquistadors - *Soldiers serving the Spanish Empire*
Desperado – *Person in a desperate situation*
Doppelgänger – *Someone who appears to be an exact reproduction of a person*
Dolores - *Dolor means sorrow in Spanish*
Drilling – *Fancy long gun with two shotgun barrels and a high-powered riffle barrel all together*
Dragoon – *Old model rotating cylinder bullet magazine requiring hand loading of powder and bullet*
Fiesta - *Celebration*

Filly – *Unbred young female horse*
Green horn – *Inexperienced cowboy*
Highwaymen - *Thief who preyed on travellers usually from horseback*
Hombre - *Man*
Jaime – *Pronounced (hi me) Spanish for James or Jimmy*
Lope – *Fast gate of a horse with a fluid leaping motion*
Non compos mentis - *Opposite of Compos mentis (of a composed mind).*
Novicia Monja of the Sacred Heart – *Novice Catholic nun of the Sacred Heart order of sisters*
Pards – *Partners, Friends*
Precociously – *Adverb for having developed abilities at an earlier age than usual*
Puedo – *I can*
Ramuda – *Herd of horses*
Revolver - *Western pistol with rotating cylinder magazine*
Runin' Iron - *Special Branding Iron for altering brands*
Sacrare! - *: from Latin consecrat- 'dedicated, devoted as sacred,' from the verb consecrare, from con- (expressing ntensive force) + sacrare 'dedicate,' from sacer 'sacred.'*
Sidewinder – *Western rattlesnake, venomous*
Sidled - *Walk in a furtive, unobtrusive, or timid manner*
Stockton – *City in Northern California between San Francisco and Sacramento*
Rig – *A horse drawn wagon or the way a cowboy wears his guns*
Stallion – *Non castrated male horse, can be very active*
Sharps buffalo rifle – *Large caliber cartridge loaded long gun*
Steer - *Castrated male bovine*
Sue – *A girl's name*
Telegram – *Message received over the telegraph system*
Telegraph – *Electric powered code message transmission system*

Telegraph Key – *Clicker device used to send telegraph messages*
Texas Rangers - *Law enforcement agency with statewide jurisdiction in Texas*
Trading post – *Business establishment, usually far away from towns and cities*
Vaquero – *Highly talented cowboy ranch hand*
Varmint – *Usually a small vector animal, term used for a bad person*
Venison sausage – *Sausage made from wild animal meat*

Long Gun

Day Of Consequence

First Printing July, 2012

ISBN: 978-1-62050-736-0

Thank you to all my friends and acquaintances
for your encouragement and generous support.

Contact Tony Sanders
tony@long-gun.com

www.long-gun.com